FURY - BOOK ONE OF TALES FROM BEYOND THESE WALLS

A POST-APOCALYPTIC SURVIVAL THRILLER

MICHAEL ROBERTSON

EDITED AND COVER BY ...

To contact Michael, please email:
subscribers@michaelrobertson.co.uk

Edited by:

Pauline Nolet - http://www.paulinenolet.com

Cover design by Dusty Crosley - https://www.deviantart.com/dustycrosley

COPYRIGHT

Fury - Book one of Tales From Beyond These Walls

Michael Robertson
© Michael Robertson 2020

Fury - Book one of Tales From Beyond These Walls is a work of fiction. The characters, incidents, situations, and all dialogue are entirely a product of the author's imagination, or are used fictitiously and are not in any way representative of real people, places, or things.

Any resemblance to persons living or dead is entirely coincidental.

All rights reserved.

No part of this publication may be reproduced, stored in a retrieval system, or transmitted in any form or by any means electronic, mechanical, photocopying, recording, or otherwise, without the prior written permission of the author except in the case of brief quotations embodied in critical articles and reviews.

READER GROUP

Join my reader group for all my latest releases and special offers. You'll also receive these four FREE books. You can unsubscribe at any time.

Go to www.michaelrobertson.co.uk

FURY - BOOK ONE OF TALES FROM BEYOND THESE WALLS

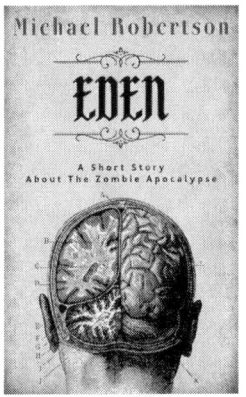

AUTHOR'S NOTE

If you're reading this, thank you for checking out *Fury*: Book one in Tales From Beyond These Walls. It's a standalone story and can be read as such. However, should you want to place it in the timeline of the main series of the *Beyond These Walls* books, it runs concurrently with book eight: *Between Fury and Fear.* The reason I chose to make this a separate book is because it doesn't follow the storyline of the main characters. Their journey continues from the end of book eight through to book nine.

Anyway, I wanted to give a little background to anyone diving in. To those who are coming from the main series, and to those who are starting on this book, I hope you enjoy Reuben's story, and thank you for giving the book a try.

Michael.

December 2020.

PROLOGUE

Lucie's legs burned. Fatigue coupled with adrenaline. Were she alone, she'd be fine. Long gone, in fact. How did she get into this situation with a fucking rookie? "Come *on*, Danko!" A thickset boy. He might be handy in a fight, but fighting had to be the last option. Why fight when you could run? "If you can't go any faster than that, you'll be dead within a week."

Three of Fear's soldiers chased them. Each one in their mid to late twenties. Experienced and armed. Two had batons like Lucie's own, while the other had a machete.

Lucie and Danko had gotten into a fight with some diseased. Danko had dropped his baton then, and before they'd retrieved it, the soldiers arrived.

Fighting every urge, Lucie held back. The boy deserved a chance. And they were only a few streets from Fury. Get to the gate and the soldiers would turn back. They just needed to—"Oh, fuck!"

Ten to fifteen diseased blocked the road ahead. A ragged mess, each of them lopsided from where their affliction had eaten away at their forms. Their jaws hung slack. The tracks of their crimson tears streaked their cheeks. Thick dry lines. They'd clearly been turned some time ago.

"What do we do?" Danko yelled through his rasping breaths.

"Don't slow down. The diseased are easier to fight than the soldiers."

"Easy?"

"*Easier*. Nothing about this city's easy."

The road bent around to the left. The alley at the end of the curve was invisible until Lucie took it, slamming her right hand against the rough brick wall to help her deal with the right-angled turn. Her palm stung from the contact. Hopefully Danko would see which way she'd gone.

Danko entered the alley a few seconds later and let out an, "Oomph!" He must have used the wall too.

At some point she might have to leave the thickset rookie. There came a time in every chase when you put yourself first. Do as much as you can and then walk away with a clear conscience. They'd taught them that in training. There seemed little point in everyone dying because of the weak link.

Fear's soldiers entered the long alley as Lucie exited. They were still twenty seconds behind Danko. Forty behind her. Enough time for her to get away. The alley's high brick walls added an echo that trebled their number. "You need to hurry up, Danko." Were it not for his lolloping gait and weak lungs, she'd be home already.

Twenty feet along the main road, she slowed her pace even more. Adrenaline flooded her system, rocket fuel spurring her on. Her muscles twitched and spasmed, daring her to go faster. She filled her lungs and let go of her breath. Filled her lungs and let go of her breath. At least she had a moment to recover. To put more in the tank for when they took off again.

A large tower block on her right, Lucie jogged towards it. Slow enough to give Danko an opportunity. His final chance. When she'd first started, she'd needed one or two.

The chunky rookie broke from the end of the alley. His mouth stretched wide, his face puce.

Lucie waved at him and pointed to the block. She ran into the stairwell.

The stairs were covered in debris, and the air filled with dust. Scant traces of the old wooden handrail clung to the rusty metal frame beside her.

She'd just passed the second floor when Danko entered. His tired, clodhopping steps called to anyone who wanted to listen. Here we are. Outnumbered and vulnerable. Come and get us! They were bleating lambs. She'd made an error bringing them here.

A shake of her head as she reached the third floor. For every step Lucie climbed, Danko ascended half the distance. She should have left him. Her voice echoed in the stairwell, "You need to hurry!"

Lucie reached the tenth floor. With the door to the roof in sight, three blue uniforms entered the building. Were they fucking with them? Surely they were faster than this? If anything, Danko had stretched his lead. Maybe they still had a chance.

At the top of the stairs, Lucie kicked open the door to the roof. The loud *crash* went off like a gunshot in the stairwell. The strong wind dragged her long hair across her sweating face. Her collar itched; her eyes burned; her trousers clung to her thighs. A carpet of small white stones on the flat roof. They wore a skin of moss. They crunched beneath her steps. She'd rolled the dice. She'd bet on the rookie. Hopefully, he fought better than he ran. For both of their sakes.

Every beat of Lucie's heart slammed through her. A ticking time bomb counting down the moments. Her stomach lurched when she peered over the edge of the tower. A long way to fall. Her baton in her sweating right hand, she widened her stance. "There's only three soldiers." She dragged her hair away from her eyes. At least she had this moment to rest. The advantage she'd have over all of them.

Danko's heavy steps mixed with those of the stampeding three. She'd take two if the rookie occupied one. But what if he couldn't?

"No." Lucie shook her head. "Don't admit defeat yet." She bounced on her toes. "You've survived in the army this long for a reason. You'll get through this."

Bang! The door flew open, driven wide by Danko. He'd appeared like a spooked cow. Wild eyes. Galloping hooves. A thick frame he battled to control. He passed Lucie and ran to the edge of the roof. Her stomach flipped, but he stopped in time. A gap of about fifteen feet separated them and the next building, which stood ten feet lower than their current spot.

"Don't tell me you're thinking about jumping?" Lucie said.

The sun glistened off Danko's sweating skin. He thew a shrug up with his wide shoulders. "We can make it."

"*You* might. I'm too short."

The thunderous call of Fear's army on their tail. At least he'd maintained his lead over them. Danko stared at the now closed door leading back into the building. He fought to get his words out. "So what do you suggest?"

"We fight them! What else can we do?"

"They outnumber us."

"By three to two. You only need to take one."

Wide eyes, he shook his head. Only the slightest gesture, but it said everything. She should have fucking left him. Lucie stamped on the white gravel. "You'd best step up." Desperation tore at her words. "Had I not waited for you, I'd be home free by now."

Danko stepped closer, drawn in by her argument. He

gulped. He looked at the steel door and halted. "But they have weapons."

"We can do this."

"Did you see that fucking machete?"

They had ten seconds before the soldiers arrived. Lucie widened her stance. She tightened her grip on her baton. They had this.

Five seconds.

Danko turned and ran. He reached the edge of the roof and boosted towards the neighbouring building. He landed on the other side like a sack of shit, his legs giving way.

"What the fuck?" Lucie threw her arms wide.

Danko got to his feet.

Lucie cupped her mouth. "I waited for you!"

"Come on, Lucie. Jump!"

The skin at the back of her knees tingled. Knees that would shatter on the hard ground thirteen storeys below. "I can't!" She stepped back from the edge. "I won't make it."

Danko backed towards the steel door leading into the stairwell of his building.

The blue soldiers were seconds away.

Danko vanished into the tower block.

The soldiers spilled out onto the roof. Three of them. They were all still armed.

Lucie took the first guard's baton to the chin. Her jaw cracked. Several teeth flew from her mouth on the back of a streak of crimson. Her legs failed her. A full-bodied kick smashed an explosion of white through her vision. Her ears rang. Her world spun.

She turned weightless from where the three soldiers lifted her. She threw sluggish kicks into the air and twisted. The soldiers were too strong.

Three men, one of them said, "You should thank us. This could be a lot worse for you."

They walked to the edge of the roof and tilted her in the direction of the opposite tower. The closed door Danko had run through.

Lucie went up, propelled into the sky by the three soldiers. Weightless once more, the tower block rushed past her. Broken windows. Empty apartments. Abandoned hope.

She held onto her scream. The only power she had left. For what good it di—

CHAPTER 1

"I'm trying to treat today like any other, Mum," Reuben said. "I'm *really* trying." He laid the bread flat and buttered it. When he'd finished, he layered on the thin slices of cheese. "I'm going for a run to see Malcolm. Then I need to get a few things from the shop." Butterflies danced in his stomach, flitting between anxiety and excitement. He took a steadying breath. "Yep, it's just like any other day." But it wasn't just like any other day. He didn't need his mum to tell him that.

Reuben shook with adrenaline. He tried to fill Malcolm's bottle with water and ended up with as much on his hands as in the bottle. "Eighteen today!" He screwed on the lid. "It always seemed so far away. I've been training hard like you said. Working at this my whole life. Dad will be so proud. That is, if they think I'm ready. I am ready, aren't I?"

Very little room to move in his bedsit, breadcrumbs covered the end of Reuben's bed from where he'd made the sandwich. He swiped them away, grabbed his shoes, and sat on the end. His mattress' old springs creaked. He tied the laces tight. "Yep, I'll just keep training. It's like any other day.

I'll go out for a run and keep busy. I'm gaining nothing waiting here."

While packing his backpack, the cheese sandwich wrapped in brown cloth, he repeated, "I'll see Malcolm on my run and then go to the shop to get a few bits. It's just like any other day."

Reuben opened his front door, letting in the fresh spring morning. The sun shone on the city. The slightest chill gave the wind teeth. He called over his shoulder as he stepped outside, "Bye, Mum. See you later." Slamming the door behind him, he took off at a jog down the main road.

By foot or on a bicycle were the best ways to travel around Fury. The city was too small for any larger modes of transport, and the streets were too tight to accommodate them. Not that they had any other vehicles. Other than their dogs, they had no tech in Fury. None of the neighbouring communities were willing to trade anything else.

The river Rend ran through the city. A two-hundred-foot bridge stretched across it. Malcolm lived beneath the bridge. He'd always said he liked it there. That he liked the cold winters and damp springs. No point in challenging the lie. What could Reuben do? Offer to let him stay in his tiny house? And what would his mum think? She called his greatest strength his biggest weakness. He was too soft. He gave people too much.

∼

Despite the enormous steel wall surrounding the city, the wind always blew hard along the river, entering through the grates beneath their fortified boundary. It dropped the temperature by a few degrees.

Out of breath from the run, Reuben picked his way down the steep riverbank with cautious steps. He unslung his backpack and removed the sandwich and drink. Malcolm always slept beneath a red blanket and always refused the offer of anything warmer. He took his daily sandwich and water, but insisted he needed nothing else.

"If sir would like to look at the menu," Reuben said to the red blanket, "I think he might be pleasantly surprised. Today, for the one thousandth, three hundredth, and eighty-seventh day in a row, I present sir with"—he held the wrapped sandwich out on the palm of his hand—"a cheese sandwich and Fury's finest bottled water."

Reuben's chest tightened when his friend didn't move. "Malcolm?"

Reuben pulled the blanket away to reveal a log.

A deep and booming laugh, it resonated in the tight space beneath the bridge as Malcolm appeared from the other side. His hair a six-inch halo of white, he had a wide grin filled with wonky teeth. Mirth shone in his brilliant blue eyes. The man walked with a stoop from so many years of sleeping rough. It masked his six-foot-plus stature. He pointed at Reuben and laughed again. "Got ya!"

While holding his hammering heart, Reuben rolled his eyes.

"I don't know whether to laugh about catching you out," Malcom said, "or to cry because no matter how many times I pull this trick, you fall for it. Do you really think you're going to find me dead beneath this bridge *every* morning?"

His face hot with his shame, Reuben shrugged. "You've told me not to worry about you, but that doesn't mean I don't. Is that such a crime?" He threw the cheese sandwich at his friend. After Malcolm caught it, he threw the bottle of water.

"Come here!" Malcolm hugged Reuben before stepping back and holding him by the tops of his shoulders. "Thank you. As always."

Reuben shrugged, avoiding eye contact, his face on fire.

"Wait a minute." Malcom gripped tighter, and Reuben did his best to hide his wince. An old man, older than his years because of his lifestyle, but he still had the strength to crush rocks in his gnarled hands. "Today's the day, right?"

It pulled Reuben's attention back to his friend. "I hope so."

"Nothing's arrived yet?"

"It's early. There's a lot of the day still ahead of us." Always looking out for other people. His greatest weakness. Trying to make Malcolm feel better about his disappointment.

"That there is. So how do you plan to spend your last day of freedom?"

"Boredom more like. And we don't know if it *is* the last day."

"Someone's fucked up big time if it isn't." Malcom sat down on the riverbank, his long legs folding into triangles, his knobbly knees pointing at the underside of the bridge.

Reuben sat next to him. "Are you sure there's nothing more I can do for you? Nothing else you need?"

Malcolm's right cheek bulged with his food. He spoke through a clamped jaw, his beard covered in breadcrumbs. "You do enough."

"I don't think I do."

"You do more than anyone else."

"That's hardly a yardstick."

"Honestly." Malcolm took another large bite, which he didn't stow in his cheek this time. His voice muffled, he said, "I appreciate everything you do for me. I don't need or want anything else."

The wind hummed beneath the wide bridge. The river churned with its fast current. It filled the silence. Gave them permission to just be.

After a few minutes, Reuben said, "Do you really think it will come today?"

"They'd be mad to not want you," Malcolm said.

And what did Reuben expect? Malcom didn't have the answers. He'd say what Reuben needed to hear.

~

THE BELL over the shop door tinkled. Reuben had spent the past few hours with Malcolm. Better he killed time with his friend than waiting at home bothering his mum. After he'd filled his basket, Patricia took his items and placed them into his bag. Bread, cheese ... "You still feeding Malcolm?"

"If I don't ..." But Reuben left the thought hanging. "Yes."

Careful not to crush them, Patricia placed the bunch of tulips in last, leaving them poking from the top of his bag. "For your mum?"

Reuben shrugged.

"You're a good boy." She smiled, dimples in her round cheeks. Because she ran the shop, she got more food than most.

He lifted his chest. "Eighteen today."

"Oh, shit!" Patricia clapped a hand to her mouth. Her green eyes widened, her hand muffling her words. "I'm sorry. I don't usually swear. But ... oh my! Today's the day, right?"

Reuben shifted his stance. He shrugged. "I hope so." What would he tell all these people if it didn't happen? How could he come back here tomorrow and make her feel better about his disappointment?

"Waste of time if you ask me." Ken, although ever present in the shop, rarely spoke. He sat in a chair in the corner, wearing the frown of someone deep in thought, but with nothing in front of him to warrant his posturing, and very little spewing from his mouth to justify it.

"No one asked you, Ken," Patricia shot back at him.

"Well, they should. I think people are afraid because I tell it how it is."

"You tell it how you see it," Patricia said. She rolled her eyes at Reuben. "There's a big difference."

"To you maybe!"

"Anyway, there's enough misery in this world without you adding to it." Patricia winked. "I swear, if they made murder legal in this city, I'd seriously consider it."

"Not if I got you first," Ken said.

Patricia moved across in front of him, blocking him from Reuben's line of sight. "Don't listen to him. You get home now. I bet you it's already arrived."

∾

Just past noon by the time Reuben got home. A warm spring day, his clothes clung to his sweating skin. He paused before going in. No sign of the delivery. His shoulders slumped. His heart heavy. It wouldn't do any good to wait outside all day. Better to face it.

Reuben unlocked his door, the hinges creaking as he entered. "Don't suppose the delivery person has been yet, Mum?" Although why he wasted his time asking ... If there had been a delivery, it would have been waiting for him. "Do you think they've forgotten about me? Or have they rejected me? I didn't even consider that." He'd considered it. He'd considered it every damn day for the past few years, but his mum didn't need to hear his self-doubt.

His mum's favourite vase, a clay pot Reuben had made for her at school years ago. He filled it with water and arranged the white tulips. The lump in his throat tightened his words. "Maybe it's a good thing. It will be nice to thank the person for delivering it when they turn up."

Reuben had spent the afternoon watching the door like a dog waiting for their owner to come home. By the time he sat down for dinner, it had gotten dark outside. No one went out after dark in Fury. Scrambled eggs and toast, he pushed it around his plate, the knot in his stomach banishing his hunger. He tried a mouthful of the rubbery egg, the salty butter, the crunchy toast. His favourite meal, but it tasted like shit today.

He shoved the plate away and blinked at the window by the door. His eyes were sore from trying to see through the darkness. "They're not coming, are they, Mum?"

The tulips remained in the vase on the kitchen worktop. He moved them so his mum could see them better. While arranging the flowers, he said, "I've done everything required of me. I'm fit. I'm healthy. I'm keen ..."

His mother's eyes sparkled. He'd drawn a thousand sketches of her over the years. His current favourite sat in the frame he'd made. Never a perfect drawing, but what would be? Perfect would be her still here now. He'd arranged trinkets and ornaments in front of the picture. A small stone heart. He'd spent the night of her funeral whittling it despite being blinded by his tears. It sat next to a wooden stick wrapped in red, blue, and yellow fabric. Acorns and fir cones, the acorns wrinkled. They'd been there since autumn. She'd died seven years previously. It still stung like it had happened yesterday. Neighbours and friends had plied him with all the usual clichés like *time's a great healer,* and *it'll get easier.* If that was the case, seven years was nowhere near long enough.

The eyes he'd drawn had taken on a life of their own. Right now they said what he didn't want to hear. But he had to accept it. "You're right." Reuben bit his quivering bottom lip. His view blurred. His voice wavered. "I'm not getting a delivery today. And it's not like they'll ever tell me why. Nothing. Ghosted. Application rejected. Now get on with your sad and lonely life. Dig holes somewhere. Work in manufacturing or agriculture." He sighed. "I wanted to make you and Dad proud of me."

Reuben drew a deep and stuttered breath. He nodded at the picture. "Tomorrow's another day. I know. Maybe tomorrow, eh?" The flame of hope in his chest flickered only to be smothered again when the shadows closed in. They'd not chosen him. To deny the reality would only prolong his suffering. No matter what tomorrow brought, his next step had to be acceptance.

Falling onto his creaking bed, Reuben rolled over onto his side, pulled his knees up to his chest, and curled into the foetal position. Tomorrow might be another day, but it wouldn't be like any other. Tomorrow, like when his mum had passed, would mark a fundamental change. The day he had to accept the life he'd spent the past several years planning, didn't belong to him. A dream that would never become reality.

CHAPTER 2

A beam of sunlight cut through the gap in the curtains and ran the length of Reuben's recumbent body. It shone from his right knee to his left eye. He dragged the covers over his face. On most other days he'd already be out of bed. But his muscles were leaden and his blood treacle.

After moving his head to avoid the glare, Reuben threw his covers to the floor and sighed. He stared at the ceiling. He'd only decorated a few months back, but it already had a new batch of fresh cracks. He sighed again. Were it not for Malcolm needing his lunch, he'd have lain there all day.

Rolling over onto his side, Reuben tutted. The vase of white tulips. His sketch of his mum. "All right," he said, throwing his legs from the bed, the tile floor cold against his bare feet. His heart beat harder than usual, punching its way through his fatigue.

"I don't know what to do with myself now." The words lifted a lump in his throat, and Reuben sat with his head in his hands. "I can see I've been arrogant to not have a plan B. While I worried, hell, I worried every day, I never really considered they'd reject me. I've done nothing but train. I've done everything expected of me and more." His voice warbled. "For *years!* Why didn't they come yesterday, Mum? What have I missed?"

Reuben stumbled across to his curtains. He threw them wide, the glare flooding the room, its brilliance forcing him back a step. He covered his face and turned away.

The same routine every morning, but today a little slower and with less co-ordination. He shuffled on tired legs to the work surface, pulled a slice of bread from the bread bin, and buttered it. He cut the cheese like he did every day. Malcolm liked it wafer thin. He filled his water bottle.

"You know what," Reuben said, pointing his butter knife at his mum, "you're right. I need to understand this. I need to know where I can improve rather than spending my time here sulking. I can't control what happens, but I can control how I react to it. And if there's still a way in, I need to understand my next steps."

Reuben tied his trainers tight. Best for him to continue running to maintain his fitness for when he won his appeal against whatever reasons they threw at him. He pulled the front door wide and stepped outside. "What the …?" A parcel wrapped in brown paper sat on the doorstep. He reached back into the house and put Malcolm's lunch on the worktop. He retrieved the package, his words riding his quickened breaths. "Look, Mum!"

Adrenaline turned Reuben clumsy as he tore at the wrapping paper. A flash of red fabric. He dug his fingers into the hole and ripped it open. A note sat amongst the parcel's remains. He read it to his mum. "We had to make a lot of uniforms in your size. It took longer than we expected. We're sorry yours is late."

The fatigue of moments before now banished. Reuben shook his head and fell onto his creaking bed. He untied his shoes, tore off his clothes, and dressed in the uniform. A perfect fit and still loose enough to wear all day, to run in, to fight in. It had razor-sharp creases down the front of each leg, and the gold buttons on the coat glistened.

"What do you think, Mum?"

The clock beside her image showed it to be ten thirty in the morning. "Shit!" Reuben said. "I have to be there in half an hour. Shit! It's okay, I can make it. I'll see you later, Mum. I'll tell you all about it when I get back." He lifted the picture and kissed his mum's smiling face. "See you later."

Two streets away from his house, Ruben pulled up and stamped his foot. "Shit!" He'd left Malcolm's lunch at home. Could he wait? But that might be his only meal today. "Fuck it!" Reuben ran back home.

~

Sweat stung Reuben's eyes by the time he reached the river Rend. He jumped down the steep riverbank and slipped, halting his fall with his left hand. It jarred his shoulder, but it prevented his uniform from getting covered in stains. Late and filthy, not a good look on day one.

Reuben's feet slipped every third step on his diagonal path to Malcolm's spot beneath the bridge. "Malcolm!" His voice carried over the humming wind.

Malcolm poked his head from under his blanket. At least he didn't pretend to be dead this morning. For a few seconds, he stared at Reuben. A glaze covered his brilliant blue eyes before he finally spoke with a gasp. "Well, well, look at you. It came, then?"

Reuben shrugged.

"This is what you've been working towards, eh?"

After handing his friend his sandwich first and then his bottle of water, Reuben said, "Uh, I don't mean to be rude, but I didn't get the uniform until this morning, so I thought I hadn't gotten in. I don't want to be late on my first day."

Malcolm shook with the effort of pushing himself up from the riverbank. He wrapped his long arms around Reuben and squeezed the breath from him. A hand gripping onto each shoulder, he bent down to make eye contact. "Take care of yourself, okay?"

Reuben bounced on the spot. He needed to go.

"I mean it." Malcolm shook him. "Take care of yourself, and remember to always put *your* well-being first. Whatever else happens, remember who you are, and don't change that for anyone or anything, regardless of the pressure you might feel. Okay?"

Compliance would be the quickest way out of there. Reuben nodded several times. "Yes. Of course. Now I need to go. I'll be back tomorrow with more food and drink."

The small amount of light beneath the bridge caught the glaze covering Malcom's eyes. His grip tightened as if he didn't want to let go. But before Reuben said something, his old friend released him. "Good luck, Reuben. May this be everything you've dreamed of."

The brief climb back up the steep riverbank set fire to Reuben's calves. His heart hammered. More adrenaline surged through him. If he moved fast, he'd get there on time.

∼

Reuben ducked down the alley between the baker's and the cobbler's. He turned sideways to scoot past a mother and her three small children. Each one of them gawked at his brand-new uniform.

Out onto the main street, the busiest stretch between him and his destination. The spectacle of his uniform slowed him down, many people watching him pass. A small boy called after him, "Thank you for your service." He'd waited a long time to hear that. On any other day, he would have stopped.

The city's gates loomed large. Thirty feet of brushed gunmetal grey steel stretching into the sky. Thick, and although far from impenetrable, they were tough enough to hold back an enemy attack while Fury mobilised.

Crowds of people gathered before them. Many with their uniform as fresh from the wrapping as his. A line of tables. Administrators sat at each one. Reuben knew the drill. He'd been here for every registration since he'd decided this was the life for him.

As the last few registered, Reuben ran up to the table, slapping his hands down, panting for breath. "Reuben Never."

The man paused, looked up, and raised an eyebrow. He had a round head shaved to the scalp, and small penetrating eyes. His mouth dragged down in a sneer. "As in *better late than ...*"

But Reuben had made it. Despite the man's disdain, he'd made it on time. He smiled, gulped against the dry itch in his throat, and repeated, "Reuben Never."

The man wrote his name. "You know you have to do at least three months service before you can leave?"

Reuben nodded.

"Fine." The man shooed him away from the table.

A minute or two to spare, Reuben joined the other new recruits. He looked at the sky, squinting against the sun. He closed his eyes and whispered, "Look at me, Mum."

CHAPTER 3

Maybe it had all worked out for the best. If Reuben had received the uniform yesterday, he would have spent the entirety of last night and that morning fretting about what would come. He'd have been second-guessing himself and would have ended up in a paralysed ball of knots. Instead, he'd had to get up, get changed, and get to the front gates before they went out for their first day.

But now he'd finally stopped and joined the other rookies waiting to meet their new team, his stomach churned. He might have looked the part, the creases down the front of each trouser leg sharp enough to cut a floating feather, but nothing would settle his butterflies. The sneers from the more experienced soldiers helped. They served as a reminder that there was nothing special about him. One of the group of rookies to start that month. He'd no doubt be a liability. They had no expectations.

Although, while a member of the bottom-feeders, Reuben stood out from the rest. Many had multiple loved ones with them, but no one came for him. No tearful mother to hold him tight. No stoic father offering him the same piece of advice they'd already given him seventeen times that month, tidbits on how to stay safe and remain alive while they were on duty. No backslapping and vociferous praise about how they did Fury proud and how they were embarking on the journey of a hero. None of the usual bullshit blown up a soldier's arse to swell their ego before they went out into the field. Because what else did they have outside the walls other than self-confidence and luck? Self-confidence, luck, and preparation. As far as preparation went, he'd done everything he could.

Many of the parents had tears in their eyes. Some openly sobbed. Mothers clung to sons and daughters like they wouldn't let go. Fathers pursed their lips in an attempt to hold it in. Above them, Fury's flag flapped in the wind. A clenched fist wrapped around a baton against a red background.

The final rookie to sign in, Reuben got shown to his team last. They stood in front of the gates, many of them in groups of five. Several of the teams had six. At the front of each team stood what appeared to be an experienced leader. The lucky rookies would be with leaders who'd served a year or more outside the walls. Just surviving for that long showed you had what it took.

Danko headed up Reuben's group. Over six feet, four inches tall and in his mid to late twenties. He had dark swollen bags beneath his sharp blue eyes. From a distance they looked like bruises. He must have done some time. Seen some things. They'd placed Reuben with a survivor. Someone to listen to and learn from.

"New boy," Danko said.

"It's, uh … Reuben."

"Uh … Reuben. Did I ask for your fucking name?"

A sharp shake of his head, Reuben dropped his gaze to the ground.

"I *hate* rookies," Danko said.

The silence pulled Reuben's attention back to the man. He glared at him like he wanted a response. "Weren't you one once?"

Danko's face turned puce. He leaned so close their noses nearly touched. The man smelled of dirt and sweat. He smelled of hard graft. Of time served. "Did I tell you to reply?"

Reuben dropped his gaze again. Even with his focus on his feet, the attention from those around burned into him. Did Danko not realise they were on the same side?

"Let me tell you something, new boy, you won't be looking this crisp by the time you've spent a few weeks outside the city. It might have been a game for you until now—"

"I don't think it's a game."

Danko's response made Reuben's ears ring. "Did I say you could speak?"

Clenching everything tight, Reuben held onto his reply.

"People die outside these walls. Frequently. You'd best be tough, and you'd best listen because I will *not* die protecting your arse out there. And I won't waste any of my team on you either. At this fucking rate, I'll be using you as bait. I'll sacrifice you first to save my good soldiers. Now pay attention because I'll only introduce you to the team once."

Danko walked down the line and stopped beside the tallest of the three women. "This is Hicks."

Hicks remained focused on the gate, her back to Reuben. She sidestepped from the line and snapped her heels together. From the back she looked like a female Danko. She had a shaved head covered in scars, and broad shoulders.

"She's done a few years less than me outside the wall. She's in her eighth year of service. There's no one I'd want more as my second in command. Don't fuck with her, new boy. Given half a chance, she'll tear your fucking throat out."

When Hicks finally turned around, she scowled at Reuben as if planning the ways she'd end him. The left side of her mouth rose in a snarl.

The next soldier in line, a short woman with long brown hair and a dark complexion. She had brown eyes and wide hips. Athletic, she'd wrestle a bull to the ground and not break a sweat. She stood five feet two at the most. Her scarlet uniform pulled tight against her thick arms. She stepped from the line when Danko introduced her.

"Hernandez. She might be small, but she's stronger than anyone I've met. She's done five years' service."

Unlike Hicks, Hernandez smiled and dipped a slight nod at Reuben. Man, did he need that. At least one of them seemed like a decent human being.

"Groves," Danko finally said. The girl on the end of the line had tanned skin and brown eyes. Where Reuben tried to make eye contact with her, she refused, her attention on the ground in front of her.

"She might be shy, but she's the brains of this outfit. You need a way out of any situation, she'll see it. She's only been on the job a few months, but she's proven invaluable to the team. You have a tough path to follow, new boy. Although—" Danko walked closer to Reuben, so close his hot breath pressed against Reuben's cheek "—I wouldn't mind betting it'll be a short path too." He looked Reuben up and down. "Did you not think to get in shape before you came here?"

Reuben drew a breath and let it go with a hard exhale. Any response would be wrong. Besides, Danko wouldn't be doing his job if he didn't make Reuben's life hard. Better to apply pressure to a rookie and see them crack now than find out they don't have the minerals when they need them most.

"So"—Danko placed his hands on his hips, a wicked smile

on his wide face—"there's something I need to know ... Why are you the only rookie with no support? Doesn't anyone care about you? Are you that unlovable?"

Aches streaked up either side of Reuben's face. His jaw clenched, he breathed in and out through his nose in short bursts. His eyes itched with the start of tears.

"Hmm ..." Danko held his chin in a pinch while he continued to fix Reuben with his icy glare. "I've hit a nerve, haven't I?" He smiled again. "What, you an orphan or something?"

Reuben pressed his lips tighter.

"You're too well turned out to have been raised in an orphanage, which is a shame because it might have toughened you up. Do you think coming here will somehow make you a stronger person?" Danko pointed at the closed gates. "That's a cruel classroom out there. Learn fast or die. So what's your story, new boy?" He stepped even closer than before.

Those around watched on.

When the tip of Danko's nose touched Reuben's, he shoved his leader in his broad chest, sending him stumbling back several steps, his arms windmilling. Danko lost his balance, yelled, and fell on his arse. Only a small number of the people there had watched on before that moment. Now every pair of eyes feasted on the spectacle.

Not only red in the face, but Danko's entire bald head turned a deep shade of crimson. He got back to his feet. A bulging vein ran from his left temple, streaking over his head. His nostrils flared, his breaths rocking through him in waves. Balled fists and a clenched jaw, Danko stepped closer. He spoke so only Reuben heard. "You've just made a *big* fucking mistake, rookie." He remained close when he shouted for the others, directing the full force of his yell into

Reuben's face. "Now get ready, troop. We're leaving in five minutes."

Danko marched off. Hicks levelled a lingering glare at Reuben before she followed. Hernandez joined the line next, and for the briefest of moments, Groves made eye contact with him. A hint of a smile played across her lips. She dipped a nod and followed the others. At least he had someone on side. A covert ally. Would it count for much? He'd be sure to find out soon. In five minutes, he'd be outside the walls, his life in the hands of the man he'd just humiliated.

CHAPTER 4

Reuben stood at the back of the line when Danko chose the front. He'd not chosen the best way to ingratiate himself to his leader, whether the prick deserved it or not.

Sarge encouraged the lined-up teams closer to the large steel gates. Grey and imposing, they did their job. They'd held strong for years.

A booming voice, Sarge clasped his hands behind his back and walked with long and deliberate steps, slamming each foot down as if trying to crack the asphalt. His hair a close grey crop that continued onto his stubbled face, a bald patch on his right cheek, where he had a round scar at least one inch in diameter. "Now, for many of you, this is nothing new. For those of you who are going out for the first time, look to those around you. To those heroes who have already served for years."

Danko made a point of leaning away from the front of the line and staring back at Reuben.

"Those with experience who do this day in and day out are the best among us. They do Fury proud every time they venture outside these walls. Know that today you're taking the first steps to becoming heroes yourselves."

It might have been an easy motivational speech for Sarge to make, but he had Reuben hanging on his every word. His heart beat harder with his swelling pride. He'd been living for this moment for the last several years. The red flag flapped in the wind. The baton-clenching fist shook in defiance of anything outside the city's walls.

Reuben straightened his back and raised his chest. He could be a hero. He could be in charge of his own team. And when he got that power, no way would he abuse it like Danko just had. Why torture rookies when he could help them grow? He'd show them the ropes. Give them an apprenticeship in serving the city like the greats before them. Make a positive difference for those following in his footsteps.

As always, Sarge's speech drew in a crowd. Reuben had been one of them on many an occasion. It had been the main reason he came here every month. He hadn't missed an induction speech in the past three years. He could probably give it himself. But he'd never seen it from this perspective. He now stood among giants. He'd become one of the city's heroes.

"Without people like you," Sarge went on, "this great city would have fallen years ago. We're great because of you, and we will remain great because of your sacrifice. So, on behalf of everyone here watching on, and everyone in the city, thank you for your service." He saluted the soldiers.

The snap of their heels came together in unison, all of them returning Sarge's gesture, the tips of their fingers on their right hands pressed against their right temples.

The *clack* of metal feet approached the gates. They carved a path, forcing the spectators aside. Only six of them today, the small robotic dogs stood about a foot tall and a few feet long. Made from steel, they might have been small, but what they lacked in size, they more than made up for with their strength. Jaws that could bite through rocks. They breathed fire. They never got fatigued because they were powered by solar panels on their backs. The robotic dogs would be beside them when they went out into the city.

Like many of the leaders, five of the dogs wore the scars of war. But one of them glistened in the sun. A rookie like Reuben. This one had come straight from the community that supplied them to Fury. Apparently they had the tech, and Fury had the food supplies. They'd come to an agreement years back. It worked. As yet, Fury still didn't have the resources or skills to make the dogs themselves.

Once the dogs had moved to the front, Sarge stamped his foot, his face reddening with the effort of his call, "Good luck, soldiers." He stood below the flag and pumped the air with a fist, a metal baton in his hand. "This is for Fury."

The soldiers raised their batons as one. "For Fury!"

Whatever had gone on with Reuben and Danko, hopefully they could put it behind them. A misunderstanding. Reuben had been a hot-headed prick and needed to apologise. He'd make everything okay. He had to. For the sake of the team.

CHAPTER 5

The chains brushed against the steel gates with a sawing whine. A rattling, shrill, and continuous note. It jangled Reuben's nerves. His stomach turned backflips. The large steel barriers twitched, shook, and then opened inwards. He'd seen this a thousand times before, but that had been from the safety of the crowd. Hard to prepare for this moment. For the first time in his life, he'd get to experience the chaos of the ruined city beyond Fury's walls.

The crack in the gates grew as if they were being driven wide by the bright sun. Its glare dazzled Reuben. An interrogator's torch he couldn't avoid. Did he really have it in him to be a soldier? Or, in a month's time, would he just be another statistic? Another rookie who didn't adapt fast enough. They might have had robotic dogs beside them, but they carried hollow metal batons. An inch in diameter and about a foot long, they were only equipped for close combat. It put them within biting reach of disease-ridden teeth.

Reuben remained at the back of his group. The opening gates had taken Danko's attention. The group on the far left moved off. Then the next group. Reuben's team went third.

Danko ushered Hicks and the others past. He waited for Reuben. "That stunt back there has waived your right to a gentle introduction. You'd best be a fast learner. For your sake. Now let's go."

Reuben froze. Sarge shrugged at him. What the fuck was he waiting for? If he'd heard Danko's threat, he hid it well. And why should he care? When they were outside the walls, Danko called the shots.

Danko overtook the rest of his team to reclaim the lead. Sarge continued to scowl. Reuben had best go now or deal with the older man's wrath. He leaned forwards, gravity giving him the shove he needed to move. He took off after the others.

The only group of the first three to enter the city at a sprint. Danko's path took them through the two teams of five who'd set off ahead of them.

When they were clear of the other teams, Danko quickened his pace. Reuben twisted and turned his way through the new recruits and their leaders. But he could match Danko stride for stride. He'd trained long and hard for this. Danko had underestimated him, and he'd see that when Reuben stuck to him like a shadow.

Groves ran ahead of Reuben, Hernandez ahead of her. If Hicks ran any closer to Danko, she'd be on his back.

When Danko looked behind, Reuben stretched his mouth wide and gasped for air, making more of the run than he needed to. Give his leader what he wanted. Pretend to be weak. Better to be underestimated.

Like every kid growing up in Fury, Reuben had climbed one of the ladders leaning against the external walls. He'd done it weekly, searching for signs of the diseased. The first time he saw one, it gave him nightmares for weeks. The thing stared straight at him. It fixed him with its ravenous crimson glare. But even then, even when he cried himself to sleep and checked out of his window in case the wall had fallen, he'd felt safe. Protected. Now the responsibility for the city's sleeping children rested on his shoulders.

The ruined buildings in the city stood much taller than he'd first thought. He'd used the walls surrounding Fury as his yard stick, the walls that had kept him safe for his entire life. But the abandoned towers dwarfed them. The glass absent from every window, crushed into the dust and dirt on the ground that glistened like glitter. Larger shards remained and occasionally crunched beneath his steps. The wind played a different symphony through the old towers than it did under Malcolm's bridge. Higher in pitch. Multi-tonal. A requiem to the memory of what this place had once been.

Cracks cobwebbed the asphalt streets. Tufts of grass sprouted through the black crust. The green shoots lay as vibrant streaks across the old white painted lines. Easy enough to imagine what the city had once been, but how many years would it take for entropy to hide the narrative? Entropy or destruction. How many more years would they be fighting their war?

Bullet holes pockmarked many of the building's walls. Scorch marks were present in equal measure. Stains from the battles between dogs and drones. A war infinitely more fierce than close combat with batons and knives.

Danko led them into a small two-storey building. It had once been someone's house. Their personal effects long gone, the building's skeleton remained. The floors were bare. A flight of grey concrete stairs led to the next level.

Despite his size, Danko flew through the old house. He tore across the first floor, hopping from beam to beam. The floorboards were long gone. He maintained his stride when he stepped on the window ledge of an upstairs window and kicked off. He caught the roof of the house next door and pulled himself up as if he were weightless.

Hicks flew across after him, as did Hernandez.

"You okay?" Groves called back.

Nice that she cared, but she didn't slow her pace. She followed the others, crossing the six-foot gap in one bound.

If Reuben slowed now, he wouldn't make it. And how far did he have to fall? One storey wouldn't kill him. Unless it broke his legs and Danko left him there. Or a drone found him. Or a diseased. A sharp shake of his head snapped the thoughts away. The ground floor visible because of the absent floorboards, he reached the window ledge and jumped, his arms flailing as he cleared the gap. The rough bricks bit into his hands when he caught the edge of the roof. His boots slipped on the wall with their scrabbling search for purchase.

By the time Reuben had pulled himself up, Danko had already crossed to the next building, this one another step higher.

The gaps grew wider, the buildings taller. His heart in his throat, Reuben followed the others. He committed to every jump. If they could do it, then so could he. Although, how high would be too high? He might run with the best of them, but …

Danko reached the last house in the line, sprinted across its roof, and jumped through a window of a hotel. He pulled into a ball to pass through the smaller gap.

Reuben followed the others and landed with a crunch of glass a few seconds later. On Groves' tail, he burst from the room. A long corridor stretched away from them, any trace of carpets or flooring long gone. Just a runway of grey concrete. Rooms without doors on either side, time had eaten away at their jagged wooden frames.

Their steps echoed in the tight space, as did Danko's mocking tone. "I hope you're not afraid of heights, new boy?"

Fuck him. "Anything you can do, Danko."

A steel fire door at the end of the hallway. A safety measure when safety measures were factored into the designs of buildings. In Fury, house fires claimed lives, but the responsibility for fire safety sat squarely with the tenant, not the builder.

Crash! Danko kicked the door so hard it slammed into the wall on the other side with a *crack.* A shower of dust fell from the doorframe.

But instead of going up like he'd threatened, Danko went down into the dark stairwell. Hicks and the others followed, Reuben last. The footsteps and heavy breaths were the only soundtrack to their workout. Those and the occasional slap from where a wall halted their descent, allowing them to turn one hundred and eighty degrees to take the next flight. What if they bumped into Fear's army now? What if they ran into the diseased or the drones? Did Danko even care?

On the ground floor of the old hotel, they charged through the foyer and out into the street. The three tallest towers in the city were behind them. The towers Reuben had studied when he stood at the top of the ladders and looked over the wall. The towers he'd underestimated from his naive perception of safety. Bathed in the buildings' shadows, Danko led them along the front of the hotel and around the side, back towards the imposing derelict towers.

Danko turned left around the back of the hotel. And thank the heavens. Reuben would go until he dropped, he'd go farther than Danko ever could, but that didn't mean he'd choose the epic climb.

His steps slammed down and Reuben's eyes burned with sweat. No need to fake his heavy breathing now. His lungs tight, he gasped as Groves turned left from the alley ahead of him.

Falling into his steps, each one slightly clumsier than the

previous, Reuben stumbled as he ran around the side of the hotel after his team.

The second he emerged from the alley, Groves grabbed him by his shirt and slammed him against the wall. She drove what little breath he had from his lungs. Her eyes were wide and her grip tight. Reuben tried to move, but she slammed him back against the wall for a second time. "Stop!"

Reuben raised his hands in submission. She let go and stepped aside. The road stretched away from them in both directions. One of the wider and straighter streets. A crack ran down its centre, a livid scar torn into it as if a great machine had ploughed the asphalt. An exposed spine of an ancient gargantuan beast.

"See those!"

Reuben followed Groves' pointing finger. The cut along the road had small metal discs planted in it. "Mines?" Then to Danko, he said, "You fucking prick! You were trying to make me run into a minefield?"

Danko levelled his icy glare on Reuben. "You pushed me. Nobody pushes me."

CHAPTER 6

They'd done a four-hour shift in the city. It had given Reuben a good introduction to the place, even if the tour guide had been a lunatic hell-bent on killing him. But after the stunt with the mines, Danko had calmed down, and they'd not seen any other action. With all the stories he'd heard over the years, Reuben had expected more. But now he'd ventured beyond Fury's walls, he'd gained a new perspective. The tales brought back by the soldiers were a highlights reel rather than a reflection of every moment in the fallen city. Who came home from a day like he'd had and talked about the hours spent walking through old buildings? Heroes weren't made from climbing through ruins like rats. But eventually they'd bump into Fear and their drones. Or the diseased. Eventually he'd have a story to justify his status as a hero.

Reuben's knuckles ached from where he gripped his baton too tight. Maybe experience would help him relax. Maybe there'd come a time where he could read the city and pre-empt danger. Until then, he'd remain on high alert.

Reuben followed Groves, who followed Hernandez, who followed Hicks, who remained as close to Danko as ever. Every step fell close to catching their leader's ankles. Had she ever tripped him? What he'd give to see that right now.

Groves, ten feet ahead of Reuben, wore the city's colours as if they'd designed the uniform with her in mind. It had been several hours since she'd saved his life, but every time he quickened his pace to get close enough to thank her, she pulled away from him. None of the group had spoken since that moment. Had it been because of the shame of what had happened and the failure of the plan? How many of them were in on it? Hicks for sure, but Hernandez? Probably not. And if Groves knew what Danko had planned, she clearly opposed it. But maybe they always behaved this way? Maybe they always marched in silence. Conversation would deny them the chance of hearing their enemy.

They walked in single file towards Fury's large gates embedded in the thick steel wall. It had been strong enough to keep Reuben safe for his entire life. Strong enough to keep people from leaving. Although, who'd want to leave the safety of their city?

Reuben's heart beat harder now than it had on the run. Harder than when he'd held onto his reaction to Danko trying to kill him. They were only one hundred feet from the gates, but what if they were ambushed now?

The ringing of chain across steel sang to them, and Reuben gasped. The gates twitched and shifted before pulling into the city, the gap widening to reveal the next shift of soldiers ready to leave.

Danko remained at the front. They maintained single file behind him. The soldiers waiting lined up like Reuben and the others had. Were there any rookies on this shift? The first team to pass them, Reuben nodded at their leader. "Good luck!"

She stopped dead, her team halting behind her. Her auburn hair scraped back in a tight plait, she had large features and bulging biceps. Her face twisted. "What?"

"I ... uh. I said good luck."

"Firstly, who the hell are you to think you can talk to me? Second, why would I need luck when I have preparation and combat skills? You rely on luck out there and you won't last a day. Third, who the hell are you to talk to me, you grinning idiot? This isn't a holiday camp, you know?" She looked him up and down. "And you're certainly not my equal. Learn your place, rookie."

"I—"

She spat at his feet, shook her head, and led her team away. "Fucking rookies."

Each of the four soldiers behind her fought to contain their mirth. Even the inexperienced one at the back snorted a laugh as they passed.

"Next time," Danko called back, "wind your neck in."

Shame set fire to Reuben's cheeks. Lesson learned. Don't speak unless spoken to. Rookies were scum. Respect came with time served.

Reuben focused on Groves' back as the next several units passed. They entered the city to a smiling Sarge. Reuben smiled back. At least someone seemed pleased to see them.

"Well done." Sarge brought his hands together with a loud *crack!* "You've made it back in one piece."

Reuben nodded. "Th—"

"Thank you, Sarge," Danko said, stepping forwards and sharing an embrace with their grizzled leader.

For the second time in as many minutes, Reuben drowned in his own shame and he physically shrank. He'd gotten ahead of himself again. He'd not earned his voice. He needed to keep his head down. Keep himself to himself and mind his own business.

"We need you all back for your next shift at two a.m.," Sarge said, slapping Danko on the back while he sent him on his way. If he noticed Reuben when he passed him, he hid it well. Any hint of the praise he'd heaped on Danko had vanished beneath his stoic frown.

After he'd passed the man, Reuben drew several deep breaths. A dampness spread through his chest. It dragged him down. The farther he got away from Sarge and Danko, the better. He needed to get home and rest. The several hours until their next shift would be enough time for him to get himself back together.

Groves remained in front of Reuben. She'd already rejected him twice, so maybe he should leave it. But she had saved his life. And what had Malcolm said to him? That he should be true to who he is. Don't give up his identity to become one of them. He owed her his gratitude. He cleared his throat and called ahead, "Hey—"

"Excuse me." A small girl stepped in front of Reuben. She clutched a dandelion to her chest in a two-handed grip. "I wanted to thank you for your service." She held the dandelion out to him.

For the first time since they'd gone outside the gates, Reuben smiled. It went some way to banishing the weight in his chest. He took the girl's gift. "Thank you."

Her green eyes spread wide. A soldier had taken the time to respond to her! She seemed to grow by several inches.

"I'll take this flower home and put it in a vase. Thank you."

The girl giggled and ran back to her mum, burying her face in her lap while her mum stroked the back of her head. She smiled at Reuben and mouthed the words *thank you*.

Groves had halted a few metres ahead of them.

"Hey, Groves." Reuben jogged to catch up to her.

She turned away from him, her focus on the ground. "What do you want, rookie?"

Matching her step for step, Reuben said, "I wanted to thank you. You saved my life back there."

"I would have done it for anyone. Danko's a prick. Bad enough that we lose soldiers in the city without people like him pulling that kind of shit."

Reuben laughed. "You know how to make a man feel special."

"I'm not trying to make you feel special. And you're a *boy*."

Her words slammed into his stomach. The final blow in a day where he'd already taken too many shots. Reuben halted. Groves continued to walk away. He filled his lungs with the fresh spring air. Go home and rest. Come back at it on their next shift. If nothing else, they had time. He'd be in this team for a while.

After several steps, Groves halted. She half-turned in his direction. "Going outside the walls always leaves me tense."

"Why do it, then?"

"Sometimes you don't have a choice. You were kind to that little girl. She'll remember that for a long time. Good job."

"It was nice of her to thank me. It helps make all the other shit worthwhile."

"Make sure you hang onto that. Look, I'll see you later, yeah? Two in the morning ... Running through the city in the dark ..." She raised her eyebrows and rolled her eyes.

"I might need help avoiding those mines again."

Groves winked at him. "*Or* you'll have to learn fast. There are no second chances with the mines."

"Learn fast or die."

Groves snorted an empty laugh. "It should be our motto."

"Hey, Groves."

She halted.

"What's your first name?"

"You don't need my first name. See you later, new kid." For the first time that day, her facade lifted. For the first time that day, she smiled.

CHAPTER 7

It didn't matter how fast Reuben ran on his way to the gates, he couldn't escape the nauseating rock in his stomach. An unreasonable time to be awake. Still dark outside, his breaths turned silver in the chilly morning air.

He'd had no breakfast, but he couldn't have eaten before he left. No time and zero inclination. Just the thought of food sent a sickening twist through him. It turned even harder when the city's gates came into view. Danko and Sarge talked and laughed with one another while they waited for the team to arrive. Or rather, waited for Reuben to arrive. Hicks, Hernandez, and Groves were already there. Of course they were.

As Reuben found his place at the back of his unit, Sarge threw his head back, fired a booming laugh at the night sky, and threw an arm around Danko. "Look," he said, "just make sure you stay safe out there tonight, okay?"

Sarge walked away, passing Reuben on the end of the line. When Reuben smiled at the man, Sarge's face fell.

"Jeez," Reuben said, a pang twisting through his chest, "could Danko be any farther up Sarge's arse?"

Groves' lips tightened and she turned her back on him. Don't drag her into that shit. She had her place in this group, and she did not want to rock the boat.

"Good chat," Reuben said. Only their second time stepping outside the walls, but he had to question it already; had he made the right choice in joining the army? How bad would the hard graft of agriculture have been? Or he could have worked in construction. But no matter how he looked at it, he needed this. He had loose threads that had to be tied.

The weight of his baton in his grip, Reuben tightened his hold. Wherever his future lay, he'd signed up for three months of service.

The chains sang, steel against steel. The gates slowly opened inwards. Reuben's fatigue got shoved aside by his adrenaline. It surged through him in waves, gripping the rock in his stomach.

Danko led them out at a walking pace. Maybe the early start affected him more than he let on. Maybe they were conserving energy because of what lay ahead?

Groves overtook Hernandez, the short and stocky woman now between her and Reuben. "Has anyone been ambushed the second they've left the city?"

Danko lifted his head and slowed. Hicks took the lead, Groves behind her.

"They tried it once," Danko said. He scanned the street as if they might try again. His heavy brow threw a mask of dark shadow across his eyes. "We dragged every one of them into the city and imprisoned them. There were seventeen of them in total. By the time we'd finished about six weeks later, just one remained. She was tough. Very tough. We let her go so she could take the message back to Fear. With the state she left in, we worried she wouldn't make it, but they've not tried another ambush since. However, it has escalated the levels of violence between the two communities. Every few years something happens that makes the war progressively worse. Turns the screw a little tighter, you know?" A flash of mania lifted his lip in an approximation of a grin. "We have to think of new and inventive ways of inflicting pain on one another."

"L-like what?" Reuben said, his heart beating as if attempting to punch its way free of his chest. "I mean, I knew things were bad between the two cities ..."

"That's what a war is," Danko said. "Taking them down before they can take you down. And hopefully scaring them enough to make them think twice the next time you meet." He shrugged. "Although, it often only serves to make them more savage in their attacks."

Heat flushed Reuben's cheeks. Sure, he wanted to protect his city, but had he been naïve with his expectations of how that might happen?

"About a year ago, Fear took the daughter of one of the higher-ups when she was serving. They worked out who she was. They reckon she's still inside Fear's walls right now. That they're keeping her alive to make sure she feels the most amount of pain for as long as is humanly possible. We have orders to show no mercy. We're to make sure every blue uniform we come across pays for the actions of those who have her." Danko led them down one of the major streets. They fanned out so he and Reuben walked side by side. The tall buildings sang like before. The wind played a symphony of misery, the wailing testimonial to a life long lost. "I'm sorry about yesterday. I went hard on you."

"By hard, you mean trying to *kill* me, right?"

The muscles in Danko's left cheek twitched, forcing his eye slightly closed. His thick chest swelled and rose when he inhaled. Although he spoke with an even tone, his words wavered with repressed fury. One spark and he'd go atomic. "I went a bit too far. I was just making sure you were up for the task. I know many a soldier who has let their team down by not being fit or fast enough. Lack of preparation could be the death of us all. I refuse to lose a team member because someone can't or isn't capable of pulling their weight."

"So I passed your test?"

"You're a fit lad, Reuben."

"Where's this sudden change of heart come from?"

"You don't appreciate it?"

"I didn't say that."

"I was talking to Sarge."

The words lifted Reuben's heart. "He told you to go easy on me?"

"No." Danko laughed and shook his head. "Sarge doesn't give a shit about rookies. Hell, I doubt he even knows who you are. But he inspired me. The way he treats me with kindness and respect despite me being a lower rank than him. It made me realise there's more than one way to skin a human."

"A cat."

"Huh?"

"The phrase," Reuben said, "there's more than one way to skin a cat."

"Why would anyone want to skin a cat?"

They'd made progress today. Best he didn't push his luck. "I'm not sure," Reuben said.

A glint on Reuben's left. The slightest flicker of movement. Shadows filled the abandoned shop, but the moon ran a silver highlight over the old metal machinery inside. Scratched and dented with age, they hadn't seen use in a long time. But something else lurked in the dark. A light where the moon couldn't reach. It shifted. Reuben gasped, jabbing a finger at the darkness. "Drone!"

CHAPTER 8

The unit paused as one.
"Shit!" Danko said. "Quick, follow me!" He led them into a large shop on their right. All of them ran at a crouch. They weaved through rows of old metal shelves. Reuben ran at the back. They reached the far corner, hunched down, and waited.

The hum of the drone's propellors drew closer. A continuous deep thrum. It grew louder, turning tension through Reuben like a tightening screw.

Light flooded the shop. Reuben's grip sweated on his baton. His throat dried. The nausea in his stomach returned. Had they already given themselves away? How the hell would they get out of this?

The surrounding shadows elongated and shortened with the drone's progress. It turned one way and then the other, searching the place with machine efficiency and logic.

Reuben gripped his baton tighter. For what good it would do against the drone's twin Gatling guns. At some point they'd find a way to arm the soldiers with weapons comparable to the ones carried by their mechanised aides.

Although, what would that do to the war efforts? Especially if one side got them first.

Danko wore a black strap with a red button on his right wrist. He pressed it and then beckoned his team to follow him. He kept low and led them to the next row of shelves, away from the drone's bright light. They moved down the length of the shop, closer to the exit.

Before Reuben could take his next step, Danko grabbed him and dragged him in another direction. The drone's light spilled across the floor where Reuben would have stepped.

Danko led them away again, back towards the rear of the shop. So much for heading towards the exit. They were rats in a maze. How long before the drone flushed them out?

The drone's hum stalked them. The light swayed one way and then the other. It knew they were in there somewhere. Reuben's throat had turned so dry he felt sick. Again! He gulped. If the thing found them, they were screwed. The Gatling guns would tear them to shreds.

They huddled in the shop's corner behind a small shelving unit. Danko raised his baton, and the others did the same. Who brought batons to a gunfight? How much of an advantage would they get with the element of surprise? Maybe it would afford them a few lucky shots? Lucky enough to walk away from this?

The drone's engines rode the stillness with a bumblebee's hum. It moved with more caution than before. It slowly searched the shop. The shadows continued to twist and stretch with its progress.

Reuben's hand shook. His whole damn body shook.

Danko held up his left hand, his four fingers and thumb splayed. He started a countdown, dropping his thumb first as he mouthed, *Five. Four. Three. Two ...*

One never came. Instead, Danko pushed down on the air

in front of him, encouraging the others to lower their weapons. And they did. All of them save Reuben.

The hum from the drone throbbed in Reuben's chest. Why were they giving up now? He tightened his grip on his baton. Danko had already proven he couldn't be trusted. Twitching spasms shot through Reuben's legs. He'd give himself his own countdown. *Three—*

Clack-clack. Clack-clack. It came from outside the shop.

The white light halted its progress.

Clack-clack.

It closed in on their position.

Clack-clack.

Several of them.

Whoosh! The drone left the shop.

The drone's white glow got banished by the brilliant orange glare of a fireball. It lit up the abandoned shop like a nuclear blast. Flickering shadows danced across the back wall. Charred dust and the strong chemical reek of burning plastic ran up Reuben's nostrils.

Out of the roaring flames came the whine of spinning Gatling guns. The stuttered burst of bullet fire. The tings of the small projectiles hitting the dogs' bodies.

Another flare of orange light. Heat flooded the old shop. Sweat dampened Reuben's brow. His clothes clung to him.

The hum and whir of the defending drone shot away from the shop and vanished down the street.

Clack-clack. Clack-clack. Clack-clack. The pack of dogs followed it.

A smile, or at least something closer to a smile than the menacing gurn from earlier, Danko held his watch up and tapped it. "It calls the dogs to our location if we ever need help. During the day, it's hit or miss whether they show up. They're often engaged in battle somewhere, but at night, they usually respond. The question is, how quickly? Tonight, we got lucky."

Reuben's thighs burned from where he'd hunched. He fell onto his bottom, sitting on the dirty tiled floor. His hard exhale puffed his cheeks as he rested his head against one of the old metal shelves. How on earth would he have come out of that fight armed with nothing but a baton? How on earth had Danko and the others lasted this long without being killed?

CHAPTER 9

They were too far into the shop for the moonlight to reach them, and now the drones and dogs had gone, the shadows won out again, throwing a dark cloak over everything. Everything except Danko's smile. His wide grin shone as if it were bioluminescent. "I knew we'd be all right."

If he knew they'd be all right, he'd hidden it well. But at least he'd gotten them out of their predicament. The dogs had been close enough, and he'd pressed the button on his wrist in time. Hardly a tactical genius, but he'd kept them alive.

The cold and hard metal shelves offered Reuben little comfort when he leaned against them. Rough with rust, the sharp edge bit into the back of his head.

Danko thrust a hand in Reuben's direction. A similar grin to the one of just a few seconds previously, although this one twitched as if it could falter at any moment. "So," he said, his pitch slightly higher than usual, "we didn't finish our *clear-the-air* chat earlier. We good?"

The others watched on. Hicks bared her small teeth, and

her green eyes narrowed. Her hand rested on her baton. She dared Reuben to reject their leader's offer.

Danko lost his rigidity as his confidence left him. Could Reuben really leave him hanging? Could he really humiliate him in front of his unit?

Reuben took Danko's hand, and, of course, Danko squeezed hard. His male pride and insecurity condensed into that one moment of contact. Real men gave firm handshakes, right? If you weren't trying to crack the other person's bones, then what were you playing at?

∾

They'd sat in the dark for at least twenty minutes. Once or twice, Reuben's head had grown heavy, and sleep had almost dragged him under. He jumped when Danko sprang to his feet and said, "Right! I think we've given it enough time, don't you? If there are any more drones, they're probably long gone by now."

They followed Danko from the shop in single file. A mazy path back through the fallen shelves. Surrounded by shadows, they focused on the moonlight-bathed street outside the shop. Reuben checked left and right for signs of the diseased.

At the entrance, Danko peered out. He scanned both ways along the road. He searched the buildings opposite. Hicks so close behind him, she'd damn near become a clothing accessory. How did he tolerate the woman? He gave her a thumbs up, which she took upon herself to deliver back to the other three like they hadn't already seen it.

Danko led the way, Hicks behind him, Hernandez running out into the street next. Before Groves could follow, Reuben said, "That was close back there, eh?"

At least she looked at him this time. She then ran from

the shop, across the main road, and down the alley after the others.

Their footsteps carried through the quiet night. Maybe Groves had been right to ignore him. Keep the noise down. Keep their wits about them. But some kind of reaction would have been nice. A smile. A nod. Then again, why did she owe him that? Maybe he should focus on himself rather than trying to elicit a desired reaction from her.

The moon shone in the cloudless sky, showing them the cracks in the road. None of them were deep enough to be ankle-breakers. Many of them sprouted wild tufts of grass. It looked like they were alone, but with so many abandoned buildings and alleyways, they had no way of telling for sure. Old tower blocks loomed over them. Pitch black inside, Reuben shuddered to imagine their enemy's eyes watching them at that moment, deciding if they had enough of an advantage to attack. How many times had soldiers come close to losing their lives and never realised it? And then there were the diseased. From what he'd learned about them, he didn't need to worry about stealth. If they saw you, you knew about it.

Reuben remained at the back of the line and followed Groves into another alley.

Danko halted at the end. No thumbs up from Hicks this time. Reuben fought to control his heavy breaths. What had Danko seen? Had Fear's army arrived? How many of them had turned up? Were they outnumbered? A growling and snarling out in the street. Reuben's pulse spiked. A diseased! He'd only ever seen them from a distance.

He shoved his way past Groves and Hernandez, and when he got to Hicks, he said, "Excuse me."

"What?" The fierce woman blocked his way and loomed over him. The side of her bald head twitched with her clenching and unclenching jaw. "What are you doing?"

"I-I …" He hadn't thought it through. But too late to back out now. "I … I've never seen a diseased this close up before."

"And that's an excuse for this insubordination?"

Before Reuben could reply, Danko said, "Let the boy see. Surely you remember your first time?" Danko winked at her.

Hicks' face turned a deep crimson. She tutted and moved over. Although, she kept the gap tight, forcing him to shove his way through, her hot breath on the left side of his face.

The creature stood in the middle of the street. One shoulder higher than the other, its left foot limp. It had a deep gash in its neck. Black with age, the wound must have come from being bitten. The mark from the attack that turned it. It looked left and right, snapping and snarling at invisible enemies. Its jaw swung with every sharp turn of its head, saliva streaking away from it. Crimson eyes, it chewed on the air with its constantly moving jaw.

Danko stepped from the alley.

"What are you doing?" Reuben said. He scanned the surrounding towers and shops. If they were being watched, they had no way of telling.

Hicks hissed in Reuben's ear, "He's doing the city a favour. While we're out, we might as well be pest control."

"But," Reuben said, "if we leave them, they could cause Fear's army a problem."

The bald woman rolled her eyes. "They could also cause *us* a problem. Now man up and grow a pair."

Danko closed in on the diseased and snapped his right arm out, his baton in his grip. An extension of his arm, he walked towards the creature, moving with a low hunch. Slow and deliberate steps, he clearly enjoyed the theatre of it. The moon shone a spotlight on him. Didn't he care about being watched? Although, from his display, maybe he welcomed it.

Hicks shoved Reuben aside, the back of his head slamming into the wall with a *tonk!* "Now get the fuck out of the way, rookie." She followed Danko into the street.

"Excuse me." Hernandez smiled and followed next. Groves slipped past, still refusing to look at him.

One last scan of the surrounding buildings. Until the enemy made themselves known, they had to assume they were alone. Reuben rubbed the back of his stinging head and took his place at the end of the line. Where the rookie belonged.

Danko put his entire body into the swing. *Crack!* Blood and saliva sprayed away from the diseased's mouth. Its legs buckled beneath it, and it folded into a sitting position before Danko kicked it over.

The diseased lay on its back, its limbs snapping with the spasms of a partly crushed spider. Its arms and legs bent back, twisting away from it as if they were independent of the beast. The creature panted heavy breaths, its wide crimson eyes blindly searching the sky. Its jaw hung loose. Broken.

Danko handed his baton to Hicks, kneeled down beside the distressed creature, and pulled a knife from his belt. Like the moon had shown Reuben the road and then the diseased, it now showed him Danko's intense focus. The flickering smile that took form and spread as he moved the tip of his blade closer to the beast's face. He slapped one of his gigantic hands over the creature's forehead, pinning it in place. His thick arm bulged with the effort of pressing down. He rested the tip of his knife against the creature's bloated left cheek and pressed harder. Thick, dark red blood leaked from the wound like tar. It slid across its pallid skin and left a glistening trail.

Reuben's stomach turned backflips. "What's he doing?"

Groves stepped away from him. How many times did she need to show him she didn't want a conversation?

Hernandez said, "What he always does. He says the diseased are good practice for when he finds Fear's soldiers. He always tries something new."

Another check around. So many hiding places. Maybe they shouldn't ask if they were being watched, but rather, by how many?

Once he'd scored an inch-long gash from just beneath the creature's eye to the top of its mouth, Danko drew another bloody cut across the first. The horizontal line of the cross ran from the beast's ear to the side of its nose. He grinned, his hand shaking as he used the tip of his knife to lift a flap of the creature's cheek away from its face.

A heave caught Reuben by surprise. It snapped through him, much to Hicks' scowling disdain. As he walked away, the bald woman hissed at him, "You need to learn to toughen up, rookie."

"But is there really any need for that?" Reuben said.

"You think Fear's army will go easier on you if you get caught?" Hicks looked down her nose at him. "And from the way you've been since you've joined us, I'd say *when* you get caught."

Reuben bit back his reply. An argument wouldn't get them anywhere.

One cheek hanging open, the diseased bit at the air with its top row of teeth. Danko's attack had left its jaw flaccid.

Danko shook with the force of pinning the thing to the ground, and pressed the tip of his knife into the creature's other cheek.

The diseased snarled and hissed. It twisted beneath Danko's pressure. The large man straddled it, kneeling on its shoulders before sitting on its chest. The diseased's weakened sternum cracked beneath the man's weight.

Danko pulled red fabric from his back pocket. One of

Fury's flags. He used the handle of his knife to stuff it into the beast's mouth.

Once he'd cut a cross in the creature's other cheek, Danko leaned close to the vile thing. All the while it snarled and twisted. It snorted and grunted like a truffling dog. They almost touched faces as he cut into the top of the creature's nose. A surgeon performing a complex operation. He worked his knife with a slow, yet deliberate sawing motion. His blade chewed into the cartilage.

Excess saliva ran down the back of Reuben's throat. He gulped. He wiped his damp palms on his trousers. He twisted where he stood. All under the watchful eye of Hicks. But he remained focused on Danko's sadistic disassembling of the vile creature. He could stomach thi—a heave lifted in his throat as if his oesophagus tried to turn inside out. No amount of swallowing or affirmations would quell his nausea.

What had once been the diseased's nose now sat as a bloody hole in the centre of its face. It sputtered, erupting droplets of blood with the thing's gasps. When Danko moved over to the beast's left ear, Reuben shook his head and walked away.

"So you don't want to see it anymore? Pussy!" Hicks muttered at him.

So what if she thought less of him? He'd seen enough. Diseased or not, this wasn't him. He wanted to protect his city and do his duty. He hadn't joined the army so he could revel in torture.

CHAPTER 10

"Right," Danko said, "that's me done."

Reuben turned around a bit too soon. He winced when Danko drove the tip of his knife into the diseased's left eye and then its right. A spasm snapped the diseased's legs rigid before they finally fell limp. Reuben's first chance to see one of the creatures up close. Hopefully, the next time he saw one, Danko would be nowhere near.

The moonlight glistened on Danko's soaked shirt. The crimson of his uniform had darkened. It shimmered with damp. He passed Reuben as he walked away from the corpse.

Despite the trauma from what he'd witnessed, morbid curiosity drove Reuben closer to the creature. His jaw fell loose and his stomach clamped. The thing's cheeks had been turned into fleshy flaps pulled wide from the crosses cut by Danko's knife. A jagged hole in the centre of its face where its nose had been. Its ears lay beside its head on either side on the sodden concrete. Blood coated its temples from where its burst eyes continued to leak, an ever-expanding pool spreading beneath the monster's head. Not satisfied with the damage he'd done to the thing's face, Danko had cut a line down the centre of its torso and had torn its chest wide. He'd spread the two large flaps of skin. Were they on its back, they would have resembled fleshy wings. Red fabric poked from the creature's mouth like the wick from a candle. Fury's flag.

"What's the point?" Reuben said.

"The point, rookie"—Hicks slammed into him as she set off after Danko—"is to get a stronger gut so you're better able to handle your time in this city. If you get any softer, you'd be liquid."

"The point—" Danko returned and raised his eyebrows at Hicks "—is to show Fear what will happen when we catch one of them. Hence the flag in the mouth."

"You'd really do that to them?"

Hicks tutted. "What do you think they'll do when they catch you, rookie? They're the enemy." She shook her head. "You have a lot to learn."

Danko walked away and the others followed. Groves behind their leader, Hernandez behind Groves. Reuben took Hernandez's lead and Hicks walked behind him.

The group progressed in silence. Overlooked by towers and shops, several of the old commercial buildings had signs and statues on top. A donut shop, it had a massive circular monument to their product that loomed large. The moon shone through its central hole. A golden M beside it. A smiling face atop the next building in the row. Some were easier than others to work out what they'd once sold. Judging by the size of their logos, they used to be important.

They passed an old stadium where they used to play a sport called football. Reuben had only heard of it by reputation, and no one could tell him the rules. But it must have been popular because they could fit the entire population of Fury inside the enormous steel structure.

Hicks quickened her pace to get closer to Reuben. It had

to come eventually. "You're soft, rookie, you know that? Time in this city will break you like a chicken's egg."

The stadium had been built with a frame of white metal poles. Rust bled through the paintwork. An auburn rash on many of the joints. Not long left for this world, a fierce storm would raze it to the ground.

"I'll be watching you," Hicks continued. "I'll be waiting for you to fuck up. And then I'll say *I told you so*. You're not cut out for this military life. Think of it as me doing you a favour. Helping you see what your too stubborn to accept."

Before Reuben replied, Groves shot him a glance. He swallowed back his response. This was an argument he couldn't win.

The stadium now behind them, they walked with their batons raised. They scanned their surroundings. The insides of buildings, rooftops, alleyways. Two shifts in and Reuben had already seen his first diseased up close. He'd gotten a better understanding of the sheer size of the old ruined buildings. A drone had cornered them. Before long, he'd fight his first battle with Fear's army. The toughest challenge of the lot. With everything else proving to be well beyond his expectations thus far, what would that inevitable confrontation teach him?

They were still several streets from home when the large steel wall surrounding Fury filled the gaps between the buildings. Its imposing gates. Grey. Solid. Immoveable. Fatigue throbbed through Reuben's legs. He'd been running on adrenaline until now.

The whine of a Gatling gun quickened his pulse. The stuttered burst of bullet fire.

Danko used his fingers to direct them into a dark alley. They followed his lead, keeping quiet by running on tiptoes.

The hum of the drone's engines drew closer. Danko stopped and raised a halting hand.

The bright glow of a headlight. It distorted the shadows at the end of the alley behind them before the drone shot past.

"I think that's enough for one evening," Danko said. He led them towards Fury at a jog, the city's gates opening up for them as they approached.

Sarge stood just inside, waiting with his hands behind his back. His brow furrowed. Crows' feet stretched away from the corners of his eyes. He'd trimmed his facial hair to a tight stubble. It exposed the scar tissue on his right cheek. A purple mess of damaged flesh. It had a story. Maybe Reuben would hear it one day.

Danko halted close to Sarge and moved aside to let his unit pass. Groves first, then Hernandez.

Reuben slowed down and smiled at Sarge, but Sarge stared straight through him. And why should he give a rookie the time of day? Still, Reuben waited. He had to try to talk to him.

"Everything okay?" Sarge said to Danko.

Danko shrugged. "Fine. We ran into a diseased. I used it as practice and left it as a warning to Fear's army."

One side of Sarge's mouth rose. He nodded. "You left a flag in its mouth?"

Danko shrugged. "We need to make sure there's no ambiguity about who did it."

Reuben stumbled forwards when Hicks shoved him in the back. "Keep moving, rookie."

Sarge glared at him before shaking his head and turning back to Danko.

A quickened pulse. His cheeks hot. Reuben dropped his head as he walked on.

Hicks remained directly behind him. "What the hell made you think you could stop and talk to Sarge?"

Reuben waited until they were far enough from Sarge and Danko. "Fuck you, Hicks."

Her eyes shot wide. She balled her fists and squared her shoulders. "What did you say?"

But Reuben quickened his pace and ran after Groves, who'd already left the military area. His back tightened in anticipation of Hicks' attack, and he only relaxed when he'd put a good few hundred feet behind him.

Groves must have known Reuben followed her, but she didn't look back.

A house on his left with a small and well-loved garden. Reuben ran over and snapped one of the pink roses at the stalk. He caught up to Groves, fell into step beside her, and offered her the flower. "Thanks for reminding me to wind my neck in with Hicks."

Continuing to focus straight ahead, Groves raised her top lip in a snarl. "You call that winding your neck in?"

"Out in the city, I mean."

"What you just did was really stupid, you know?"

"Borrowing a rose?"

"Making an enemy of Hicks. She's an arsehole. When she takes a hold of a grudge, she'll remain locked on like a guard dog on an intruder's crotch. And you stole the rose, you didn't borrow it."

"So you're talking to me now, then?"

"You've seen what they're like."

"What's that supposed to mean?"

"Danko and Hicks. When around those two, I've learned it's best to just do your job. Follow their orders. Speak when spoken to. Otherwise, shut the hell up. The aim is to end the shift alive. Nothing else matters. Especially not passing the time with inane chat."

"Inane?"

"When you're outside those gates, anything that doesn't

count towards keeping you alive is inane. You'd do well to follow my lead."

The sky had turned from black to dark blue, ushering in a new day. A man dragged a large cart behind him filled with milk. A woman assisted him. She took the bottles from the back one at a time and delivered them to the houses. They paused when Reuben and Groves passed, both of them dipping their heads. Both of them spoke in a whisper appropriate for this time of day. "Thank you for your service."

"You're welcome," Reuben said.

Groves continued to focus on the road ahead.

"So where are you going now?"

"It's four in the morning, where do you think I'm going?"

"Stupid question, right?"

Groves shrugged. "My dad always said there was no such thing as a stupid question, just stupid answers."

"In that case, how about I ask another one?"

"I didn't say I agreed with him."

For the second time, Reuben held the pink rose towards Groves. "Will you go on a date with me?"

"No."

"Okay, I'm sorry. I must have misread the signals. Shall I leave you alone? I don't want to harass you."

When Groves didn't reply, he said, "If you want me to leave, say."

Another pause.

"Will you tell me your first name?"

"No."

"If I guess your first name, will you go on a date with me?"

The slightest pause. The moonlight caught the shine of her glossy black hair.

"Is that a yes?"

Groves waited for a few more seconds before she said, "It ain't Rumpelstiltskin."

"I didn't say it was."

Groves shrugged. "You don't want to bother with me."

"Can I be the judge of that?"

She shrugged again.

"So, who do you live with?"

"My little sister, Annabelle, and my dad."

"That's it?"

Until that point, Reuben had felt the need to fill the silence. This time he waited.

"I used to have a big sister called Reecy," Groves said. "She was six years older than me. She died while serving in the military. Fear's …" She cleared her throat, the cough going off like a gunshot in the still morning. "Fear's army caught her."

"And your mum?"

"Cancer. Years ago."

"Sorry to hear that."

"It happens."

"I don't mean to sound insensitive."

"Don't, then."

"But if your sister joined the military and died …"

"What made me join?"

Reuben shrugged.

Groves' dark eyes appeared to darken further. "You get good rations for being in the army. Dad can't work because he injured himself fighting for the city years ago. If I don't bring in rations, we don't eat. Maybe I'll die in the line of duty too."

"And that doesn't frighten you?"

"Of course it does, but because Dad's served in the military, if he loses two kids to the war, he'll get a state pension. Rations until the day he dies."

"He doesn't get a pension anyway?"

Groves laughed. "You think the city would look after him now he's of no use to them?" She shook her head. "No, he was a hero for as long as he was active, but now he's a washed-up has-been. He has to sacrifice his children's lives if he wants anything back from the city. But it is what it is. And me serving means Dad and Annabelle will be okay. Whatever happens, they either get my rations from being in the military, or government rations when I die."

"I hope it's your rations."

Hard lines streaked Groves' brow.

"You're a good person, you know that?"

"So because roses didn't work, you're going to try flattery instead?"

"Just calling it how I see it."

Groves moved away a step, heading in a different direction. But before the gap between them grew too large, she reached across and took the rose. "Sleep well, yeah?"

Reuben stopped in his tracks, a smile playing with the sides of his mouth. "You too."

"Oh, and don't expect me to be all chatty when we go out tomorrow."

Reuben grinned. "Night, Groves. Sleep well."

CHAPTER 11

Reuben had made so many cheese sandwiches, he'd honed the process down to a fine art. Just enough butter to cover the bread. The cheese thick enough to add a salty tang, but not so thick it became overpowering. He cut diagonally across the sandwich, wrapped it in a cloth, and left it on the work surface next to a bottle of water.

"So, I've been wanting to tell you about a girl I've met," he said to the picture of his mum. The white lilies had started to wilt in their vase. "I think you'd like her. She's got a big heart and she's fiercely loyal. She pretends to be mean and moody, but it's a front. A way of staying alive out in the ruined city. She saved my life the first day we went out." He changed into his uniform, sitting on the bed as he pulled on his trousers.

"The other people in my team are all right. There's Danko, our leader. I'm not one hundred percent sure about him. At first I thought he was an arsehole, but he seems like he wants to be a good person, it's just something he struggles with. He has a lot of demons. Hicks is a weapons-grade arsehole. A nasty piece of work. She's a sadist, and I feel like I have to constantly watch my back when she's around. The other person is a woman called Hernandez. I like her." He pulled on his jacket and stood up. "She shoots straight. What you see is what you get. She seems like she's doing the job for the right reasons. She's a good soldier who wants to help. She has no interest in becoming a hero or taking anyone else down, unlike Hicks."

Lifting the sandwich and water from the side, Reuben said, "Anyway, I need to see Malcolm and then get to the front gates. Love you, Mum. See you later."

∼

THE STEEP RIVERBANK burned Reuben's already sore legs as he descended. Before he'd gone outside the walls, he'd believed he had the stamina to cope with whatever they threw at him. Who knew it would only take two sessions coupled with an erratic shift pattern to show him different? How would he feel at the end of the first month?

Malcolm got up when he saw Reuben, walked over to him, and wrapped him in a tight hug. "I was wondering if I'd see you today."

"You were worried I'd died already?"

Malcolm looked at his feet. "The diseased have quite a reputation. Run into a horde and you're screwed."

The image of what Danko had done to the diseased dragged Reuben's thoughts away from the conversation. He caught them before they went too far, laughed, shook his head, and said, "You don't need to worry about me. I'm doing well." His voice wavered when he added, "Honestly."

After taking the sandwich and drink, Malcolm nodded his thanks and sat down again on his red blanket. A mild afternoon, but the wind still found its way under the bridge. Eating his sandwich with one hand, Malcolm pinned down his wild hair with the other. "So how's it going?"

Reuben's uniform flapped in the breeze like Fury's flag on the gate. The flag in the diseased's mouth. Its tacky and exposed sternum. Its burst eyes …

"Reuben?" Malcolm raised his eyebrows.

"Yeah." Reuben nodded. "It's going okay."

The smile fell from Malcom's face.

"I like what I'm doing. I feel like I'm helping Fury. That I'm a part of the team keeping the people safe."

"But …?"

"Not everyone in my unit is someone I'd choose to spend time with. There are two of them in particular. They've served for quite a few years already."

"Maybe they've forgotten why they joined. Maybe they've forgotten who they are. I'd imagine that could happen easily."

Reuben nodded. "Yeah, I'm sure you're right." The wind picked up, howling beneath the bridge. "But what can I do about it?"

"You can make choices."

"What choices?"

"You might not have control over the situation, but you can control how you react to it. Maybe they need someone like you around. Someone with enthusiasm. A fresh reminder of what the military does for the people in this city. Help them remember their purpose, you know? Show them why they joined up."

"I think our leader, Danko, has it in him to remember. But Hicks …" Reuben pointed at his temple. "She's fucked in the head. From what little I know of her, I'm not sure she was ever normal. I'm not sure she ever signed up for the right reasons."

"And how are the rest of your team?"

"Huh?"

"You said two of them are bad eggs. A unit is typically five people, right? What are the other two like?"

"Hernandez is nice. She's straight down the middle, you know? Normal. Kind. Supportive. A good soldier. I like her. And Groves—"

Malcolm shifted on the blanket to make himself more comfortable. He leaned towards Reuben and grinned. "Tell me about her."

"How do you know it's a her?"

"You're into women, right?"

"What's that got to do with anything?"

"You're blushing."

Reuben cleared his throat. "Uh … um …"

"Don't be shy. It's okay."

"She's nice. Although she's a tough nut to crack. I think she feels the same way about me."

Malcolm got to his feet again. Breadcrumbs in his beard, he clapped his right hand on Reuben's shoulder and lowered his head to force eye contact. "You're doing the right thing. Just stay strong. Whatever you do in life, there will always be arseholes. Those people get found out. Let them be the masters of their own undoing."

Reuben hugged Malcolm again. "Thanks. I've got to get going. I'll be back tomorrow, okay?"

"Don't feel you need to."

"I want to. See you tomorrow."

"Take care, son."

The words slammed into Reuben's chest. His eyeballs itched. He rubbed them. No one had called him son before. He coughed to clear the lump, his voice still weak when he said, "Thanks, Malcolm."

∼

"This is only your third patrol, but I wanted to say well done to all the rookies. It's not uncommon for us to lose one or two of you in the first few days." Sarge paced up and down in front of the units, his usual long strides, his hands clasped behind his back. Twenty groups of five, they lined up in teams in front of the gates.

Sweating from his run over there, Reuben stood at the back of his unit and tugged on his thick collar. The uniform might have looked the part, but they could have used a thinner fabric. Like how they'd lined up on the first day, Danko stood at the front with Hicks attached to him. Hernandez next with Groves behind her.

"I want you all to remember why you're here and why you're doing this." Sarge slapped the back of his right hand against the open palm of his left, stressing each point with a sharp *crack!* "It's people like you keeping Fury safe. And it's people like you who, when the time's right, will help us win control of the ruined city and crush Fear for good." Sarge raised his fist with a baton in his hand, mimicking the flapping flag on the wall above him. His face reddened when he shouted, "For Fury!"

The soldiers copied Sarge's actions and chanted as one. "For Fury!"

The chains sang, adrenaline flooding Reuben's system. The enormous gates twitched and shook. They opened inwards, the full force of the afternoon's low sun dazzling him. A group of eight dogs charged out first, their metal feet clacking against the cracked asphalt as they disappeared into the city. Many of them were battered from their time served. One or two were lame. They soon disappeared from sight.

The first group on the far left set off after them. Unlike the first time they'd left the city, every unit ran, their footsteps slamming down in time. The next group followed them out.

Fifth in line that morning, Reuben followed Groves out of the city when their time came. The units ahead of them forked off one by one. Some turned left while others turned right. They'd find Fear's army and flush them out. Eradicate the fuckers.

∼

LIKE HE'D DONE on the first day, Danko led his unit through the skeleton of an old two-storey building up to its roof. A line of similar structures, they had flat roofs and were so close to one another it made it easy crossing from one to the next. The three tall towers, one of the most recognisable set of landmarks, dominated the skyline in the distance.

They'd seen the city's old football stadium on their previous shift. Now, as they made their way from rooftop to rooftop, they passed another sporting venue. An arena. At some point, the front of the building would have been covered in glass. Only the metal framework remained, and the ground sparkled as evidence for what had once been. A massive statue of a man stood hunched over on the building's roof. Thirty feet tall, maybe even more. He held a stick of some sort. Reuben shielded his eyes against the sun to help him see better.

Danko slowed down on the next building, allowing his unit to catch up. All of them breathed heavily from the run.

"What did that place used to be?" Reuben said. He shivered from the line of sweat running down his back.

"What does it look like, rookie?"

Even Danko ignored Hicks' venom. He smiled, although the gesture looked like he'd borrowed it from someone else. Had he started modelling himself on Sarge? Did he have plans to take over his job at some point? What would that look like? "They used to play ice hockey in there."

"*Ice* hockey?" Reuben said. "Bit warm for ice hockey, isn't it? Especially to erect such a large arena for it. How many times a year did they have the right weather to play that?"

"The place used to have windows, so it was better sealed. They kept the temperature in there cold enough for the ground to remain frozen. They used to wear skates, which were boots with blades on the bottom. They'd hit a small disc called a puck into their opposition's goal. It was a violent sport, and it wasn't unusual for a game to turn into a brawl."

"Shame they don't play it anymore." Hicks raised her eyebrows at Reuben.

Reuben kept his attention on his leader. For the first time since he'd met him, Danko seemed almost human. "How do you know all this?" Reuben said.

"My old man told me. He's a historian. He can't understand why I'd want to be a soldier. I dunno, we don't see eye to eye that often, but he knows some fascinating ..."

When Danko trailed off, Reuben followed his line of sight. Two people ran through the city. A man and a woman. They were in their thirties. They held each other's hands as they ran. "Who are they?"

"Trespassers." The ice had returned to Danko's tone. He dropped into a crouch.

"But they're not from Fear. Well, they're not wearing their colours."

"Which makes it even worse. At least I understand why Fear are out here." Danko's face twisted. His venom drove spittle from his mouth. "Who the hell are they to think they have any right charging through *my* city?"

Hicks grinned while Hernandez and Groves stepped back from their enraged leader. Reuben followed suit, the gravel on the roof crunching beneath his retreat. "What are you going to do to them?"

Danko remained focused on the two. "You saw my practice run yesterday."

"But I still don't understand what they've done wrong."

"Are you deaf or something?" Hicks cocked her head to one side. She spread her eyes so wide her eyeballs damn near fell from her face. She bared her small teeth, her thin lips peeling back. "They're trespassers. This city belongs to Fury."

Danko ran away from them towards the edge of the building. When he jumped off, Reuben's stomach flipped … until he reached the edge himself and the fire escape leading to the ground. Danko had already reached the first floor, Hicks on his tail. Danko leaped over the railing, falling the final ten feet. He landed with a slap against the cracked asphalt.

Where he'd always been last, Reuben ran ahead of Groves this time, following Hernandez after their crazed leader.

Danko jumped through the glassless window of the old building they'd been standing on. He weaved through the rusting and twisted metal frames, the skeleton of the shop's furniture. He waited by the window leading out into the road. The sunlight shone into the building, but they were hunched down and hidden from sight.

When they'd all caught up, Danko said, "We need to be patient. We're tigers in the grass. We wait for our prey to come to us rather than chase it all over the city. We'll get our moment to strike."

Reuben's heart pounded and he shielded his brow as he watched the couple run towards them. Towards them and away from something. But what? Maybe they were being chased by their imagination. Driven by fear, maybe they knew what it meant to pass through this abandoned city. Maybe they had no other choice. They held hands as they ran. They frequently checked back. What harm were they doing anyone? Why did Danko want to take them down? Did he want another practice run? But these two weren't diseased. They had rights.

Danko, Hicks, and Hernandez all in front of him, Reuben held back with Groves. They weren't the decision makers here. The knife Danko had used on the diseased poked from the back of his belt, the wooden handle stained with blood.

Reuben leaned too far forward to watch the fleeing couple and nudged Danko. Their leader turned around and shoved him. He stumbled and his ankles slammed into a piece of old furniture. He tripped, his coccyx taking the impact of his fall. Fiery streaks twisted through his back, which he rode out with heavy breaths through his nose while biting down on his bottom lip.

"What are you doing, new boy?" Danko said. "Give me some space, yeah?"

It took Reuben a second to get to his feet. He stepped closer to his leader while rubbing the base of his back. "Uh, Danko."

"What?"

Hicks and Hernandez also turned Reuben's way. Hicks wore a similar expression to Danko. She also wanted to tear his fucking face off. Reuben held up Danko's knife. "You dropped this."

The sunlight reflected off the shiny blade, Reuben having dragged it on his trousers to clean the blood from it before he handed it over. The glint briefly attracted the attention of the woman running through the city. She threw the slightest glance their way.

Reuben handed the knife to Danko handle first, who tore it from him.

Groves' eyes widened ever so slightly. Had she seen what he'd done?

"Fuck!" Danko stamped his foot. "They've gone the other way. Fuck!"

"Let's chase them." Hicks stepped out into the street.

Danko pulled her back and shook his head. "Tigers know

when their prey is worth pursuing. Those two will be long gone by now. We'll only tire ourselves out."

Hicks might not have twigged, but she glared at Reuben like she wanted to lay the blame on him. If she ever worked out what he'd done, she'd take Danko's knife and use it to cut his damn throat.

CHAPTER 12

Hicks lunged at Reuben, leading with her pointed finger. "It was *you!* I know it was." Her thin lips pulled back, and she spoke through her clenched little teeth. "*You* did something."

At least Reuben had learned from his first fall, sidestepping the woman's advance so he didn't trip a second time.

Danko got between the two and pushed Hicks away. "Will you shut up? Reuben's done nothing wrong. What the hell are you talking about?"

Reuben's pulse quickened when Hicks shook her head. Groves' attention burned into the side of his face. Had she seen what he did? Would she rat him out?

Leaning around Danko, Hicks pointed at Reuben again. "You did something. I know you did."

"All right." Danko threw his arms out in an exaggerated shrug. "If you're so certain he's to blame, tell us what he did?"

"I dunno …" Some of the tight wind fell from Hicks' thick upper body. She had a lot of power in her shoulders. She'd tear Reuben apart.

"So what's your point?"

"I *know* he did something."

"So you know he did something, you just don't know what? And you want me to act upon that? Surely you can see the situation you're putting me in here? What do you expect me to do?"

"I expect you—"

Danko showed her the palm of his hand. He pointed towards the sporting arena with the hockey player on the roof. The shop they were in formed part of a street. The street opened onto a patch of concrete in front of the massive structure. A plaza. Somewhere the crowds would gather on the day of a big game. How could any group of strangers get so close to one another without tearing each other apart? What had this city looked like when people lived here in peace?

The couple might have moved on, but a soldier in a blue uniform now walked through the space. Mirth rumbled in Danko's baritone purr. "This is even better." He hopped over the low wall and out into the street.

Hicks stepped on the wall to follow him, but Danko showed her his halting hand again. "You lot wait here. Let me draw him in first. We'll ambush this motherfucker and make him pay for the sins of his city. Hernandez, I want you to lead the ambush."

Where her face had been puce before, Hicks now damn near glowed, her head a throbbing beacon of incandescence. Reuben moved another pace away from her. He might have had Danko's backing, but how long would that last, and did it count for anything with her in this state of mind?

Before Danko ran off, Hicks reached out from the shop and dragged him back. A little too rough, she had his shirt gripped in her fist. "What about me?"

Danko stared at where she held him. His tense jaw twitched.

She let go.

His tone might have been level, but an unspent rage lay beneath Danko's words. "Don't make problems for me, Hicks."

She withdrew into the shop. A scolded insubordinate, she returned to the shadows where she belonged. Reuben took another step away from her.

As Danko crossed the street, Reuben's stomach swelled with his deep inhale. The diseased Danko had caught slammed through his mind. His arsehole twitched. It had been bad enough to witness what their insane leader did to one of those creatures. Could he stand by and watch it happen to a person? No one deserved that. Enemy or not.

Using the buildings along the opposite side of the road as shelter, Danko drew closer to the plaza.

Hicks sidled up to Reuben, and he jumped when she hissed, "I promise you, rookie, I *will* make you pay for this. I know you just scared that couple away, and whatever happens, I will find out how you did it. Then we'll see whose side Danko's on."

"Hicks," Hernandez said, "we have more pressing matters right now. Can you please shut the fuck up?" Hernandez spoke again before Hicks could. "Right, are you lot ready? We're going after Danko." She counted down with her fingers. "In three … two …" She dropped her last finger and stepped out into the street, Hicks as close to her as she got to their leader.

Groves stood aside for Reuben to go next. He stepped out onto a piece of glass. It broke with a gentle pop.

They followed Danko's path, using the shelter of the buildings on the opposite side of the road to remain hidden. While the insides of each derelict shop had different layouts, different twisted wrecks of what had once been inside them, they were so alien to Reuben he couldn't tell what their business had once been. Maybe he'd meet Danko's father one of these days and get him to give him a history lesson on the place.

Danko broke from cover and charged across the plaza, his baton ready. The soldier had his back to him.

Only twenty feet separated them when the soldier turned around. His jaw fell.

"Now," Hernandez said.

Were it one on one, the soldier might have stayed and fought. But he looked past Danko at Hernandez's charge and ran.

His baton raised, Danko ran after him and yelled, "Don't let him get away!"

The blue soldier moved fast and opened up a lead. But he didn't move as fast as Hernandez. She overtook her leader and closed the gap on the retreating enemy. Short and squat, she charged like an enraged rhino.

Fear's soldier had too much of a lead. They had no chance of catching him. Were it up to Reuben, he would have stopped there. But Danko needed this. Hicks needed this. And what harm would it do to chase a lost cause if it made them both feel like they were doing something?

Hernandez followed the soldier down an alley, Groves behind her, Reuben next. Hicks and Danko took up the rear.

The soldier had stopped at the end. His smile robbed Reuben and the others of their pace.

Ten to fifteen soldiers appeared behind their comrade and blocked the exit.

Footsteps behind them, Reuben turned around. A woman in Fear's blue uniform had closed off their escape. She had as many soldiers with her as the man at the other end.

"Are you lot new or something?" the woman said. "Is this your first time outside Fury's gates?"

"Fuck you," Hicks said. She spat on the floor in the woman's direction.

Cackling laughter filled the alley and subsided a few seconds later. The woman tutted several times, a metronomic click locked in with her shaking head. "You took the bait a little too easily there. I almost feel sorry for you. Hell, I feel sorry for myself. I do so love the thrill of a hunt. This feels more like bullying." She slapped her baton against her open palm, closing down on them with slow and deliberate steps, her army behind her. "I suppose we'll just have to make the punishment even more extreme. We have to get our kicks somehow, right?" She raised her baton and released a tongue-rolling shriek. The others joined in with the shrill war cry.

CHAPTER 13

The army's wave of sound hit Reuben and forced him back a step. They screamed, roared, and yelled as they flooded into the alley from either side. The rumble of their thunderous stampede shook dust from the close walls of their now prison.

Hicks raised her baton higher and shook with the force of her yell. "You think we're scared?"

Reuben's stomach clenched. His breaths shortened. His heart raced.

Danko looked one way and then the other as if he couldn't believe they were trapped.

A fire escape up to their right. The bottom flight of stairs were missing. Groves kicked off from the left wall and boosted for the metal structure. Her grip true, her momentum turned into a pendulous swing. She shook with the effort of pulling herself higher. She kicked her legs to aid her climb.

Danko followed. Hicks next.

Hernandez stood proud, but her features faltered and her eyes watered.

A matter of feet to go before the Army were upon them. Reuben bent down and linked his fingers. "Let me boost you."

Even in that moment, with the imminent threat to their lives, Hernandez smiled, nodded her thanks, and stepped into his grip. The dirt on the bottom of her boots cut into his hands, and he yelled with the effort of launching her. As he sent her up, Danko leaned down and caught the back of her coat.

The army less than ten feet away, Reuben copied Grove's route and boosted from the wall opposite. He caught the rusting fire escape, the rough surface biting into his grip, and trembled with the effort of pulling himself clear. One of Fear's soldier's batons slammed into his right heel. His legs swung out, and the strength left his upper body. As his grip weakened, Hernandez and Groves grabbed an arm each and dragged him to safety. The leather of his boots saved him, but his ankle throbbed from the blow. It stung when he tested his weight. It stung, but it held. Nothing broken.

The true extent of Fear's army was below them. A hundred soldiers, maybe more. They packed the alley from both sides. The first couple who tried to climb after them felt Hicks' wrath. A baton across the side of the head. Two hollow *tonks!* They fell back into the crowd. They weren't getting back up again in a hurry.

The rest of the army snarled and hissed, but they didn't try to climb. It gave Groves the chance she needed. Her feet slammed against the metal steps. The rusting staircase shook as the others followed. On the roof, Groves jumped the alley to the building next door.

At the back of the line, Reuben made the leap across. Small white stones covered the flat roofs stretching away from them. Groves led the way from one building to the next, taking the narrow alleys in her stride.

Several buildings behind them, Groves, Danko, and Hicks moved to the left side overlooking the road. Reuben and Hernandez ran down the right. They'd opened a lead on the blue army, who spilled from the alley like wasps from a burning nest.

Six or seven rooftops later, they pulled back into the centre. Reuben said, "How's it looking on your side?" He pointed to where he'd just come from. "We have about fifty soldiers down there."

"Same," Groves said. "But at least they're divided. Follow me."

Groves moved back over to the left. Once she'd cleared the next alley, she jumped and landed on the building's fire escape with a *crash!* Three loud splashes as Danko, Hicks, and Hernandez followed. Reuben leaped last. The entire stairway shook with his clumsy touchdown.

The army on the ground roared.

Down one flight of stairs, Groves vanished into the building through the first-floor window. The others followed. Several knives and rocks clanged against the stairs. One flew across the front of Reuben's face, the tip an inch from embedding in the side of his head.

As sparse as the other buildings in the city, the furnishings had been long since destroyed. The floorboards had rotted away. Thick beams remained. The building's ribcage. They hopped from one to the next, crossing to the other side. Reuben tried not to look down.

One window in each wall. Groves ran for the one on their right. The beam she'd chosen was two inches thick at the most. She travelled several feet along its length, her arms thrust out for balance. The window faced the building they'd just crossed. A narrow alley separated the two. Groves stepped onto the window ledge, leaped, and pulled into a ball.

Danko and Hicks followed. Hernandez slowed her pace. The dusty air caught in Reuben's throat when he yelled, "Don't doubt yourself."

Hernandez sped up again and boosted from the window seconds before Reuben followed her. Landing two-footed, the slap of his clumsy leap echoed through the empty building.

Groves had already vanished through the window on the opposite side. Hicks had gone too. Danko next, followed by Hernandez. Reuben continued after his team.

This time, when Reuben landed, he turned back. He poked his head from the window and looked both ways. No sign of the army. Maybe Groves had bought them enough time. Maybe.

Back to the fire escape that had saved them minutes before. Groves leaped onto it before she vaulted over the railing to the ground. Danko followed. He managed the one-storey fall like a lump of wet clay. Thankfully, he got to his feet again. No way would they be carrying him out of there. Seconds mattered.

Hicks, Hernandez, and Reuben all landed. They were back where they started. Back in the alley they'd been trapped in. Groves led them away again.

At the end of the line, Reuben burst from the alley last, and the roar from Fear's army answered his silent question. Yes, they'd been spotted.

His lungs tight, sweat damn near blinding him, Reuben willed on his tired limbs. It didn't matter how many times he'd run through Fury and how varied the routes, nothing could have prepared him for this. Hard to replicate the adrenaline-fuelled fear for your life.

In the alleys opposite, Groves turned left and right as she took one turn and then the next, the mazy route enough to make anyone dizzy.

Ten to fifteen turns later, they burst into a vast car park. The army's thunderous pursuit remained on their tail. Impossible to tell how close.

Like the major roads, cracks stretched across the asphalt. Cracks lined with green mohawks of grass. Nature had patience. It would win out against its human-made oppressor. The car park served the once-customers of the shopping mall. If Reuben had read Grove's trajectory correctly, they were heading straight for the massive building. Made from the same steel as the football stadium, it too bled rust from its metal skeleton.

The first of the blue army appeared behind them. Nowhere to hide in a space like this. But they had enough of a lead. Hopefully.

The footsteps told Reuben all he needed to know. Fear was on their tail. They spread out as they burst from the alley. They'd tear them to pieces if they caught them. He remained fixed on their destination.

Groves, still the quickest, shot into the mall. Reuben ran in second. A white tiled floor stretched away from them. Spiderweb cracks dominated each square, the tiles decorated with black lines of dirt. Many more were missing altogether. Only slight dips where they'd once been, but they dipped enough to demand his focus. Enough to unsettle his balance. One bad fall could end everything.

The acoustics of their escape altered once more for having a roof over their heads. The pitch of their steps lifted when they reached the metal stairs in the centre of the mall. They led to the first floor. They had sharp right-angled edges that'd rip a shin to shreds. Groves continued to guide them like she had a plan.

The other three were close behind. Fear's army was yet to enter the place.

Groves ducked into a shop on their left. She weaved

through the metal frames. Old clothes racks, the years eating into their once chrome surface. Like the alleys, she led a mazy path. Designed to leach the pace from their pursuers and hopefully buy them a little more time.

At the back of the shop, Groves kicked open a steel door with a *crash!* Reuben stumbled through after her. The concrete stairwell caught him unawares. The ground vanished beneath him. His momentum carried him down the first few steps. He fought to master his balance, his feet twisting as he rode out the half-fall. He slammed into the wall shoulder first. It jarred his body and forced the wind from him with a bark. He turned and followed Groves down the next flight.

Hicks, Danko, and Hernandez remained close. All of them gasped for breath.

A set of double doors at the bottom opened into a car park. Just as Reuben ran through, the first of Fear's army broke into the stairwell two floors above.

Reuben held the doors for the others. Hernandez through last. He slammed them shut behind her and threaded his baton through the handles. It might not buy them much time, but, right now, he'd take what he could get.

Hicks spun around and faced the doors. Her eyes wild, her thin lips peeled back to reveal her small teeth. The light from outside found its way into the car park and glistened on her sweating skin. "We should fight them."

Reuben passed her, chasing after the others. Hicks could fight whomever she wanted as long as she didn't expect backup.

A short incline led them from the underground space. They ran across a smaller car park on the other side of the mall. Groves led them into an old residential area. Rows of compact terraced houses comprised their next labyrinth.

Shards of glass littered the ground in the tighter streets. Every window had been smashed.

They ran for a few more minutes before Groves finally came to a halt in a small courtyard.

Hicks charged in last and stopped.

Reuben hunched over, his hands on his knees while Danko slapped Groves' back. "Well done." He took a second to catch his breath, but his next words were cut off by the low hum of drones' propellers heading their way. Danko pressed the button on his watch, for what good it would do. The dogs were always too busy during the day.

Groves raised her eyebrows, her cheeks puffing out with her exhale. She shook her head and took off.

Hicks held back. "So we're going to run like cowards again, are we? I say we stand and fight." She soon followed when they left her on her own.

The route more complex than any of the others. And it had to be. The blue army's distant screams melded with the hum of their mechanised predators. Groves led them through the old housing estate. Left, right, left, left, left, right, right. For all Reuben knew, they ran in circles. But he couldn't do a better job. And he trusted Groves with his life.

Groves paused again. Reuben reached her first. She'd stopped on a metal disc. Two feet wide, it led to the sewers. An old fence stood on Reuben's right. Made from rusting iron railings. Horizontal bars ran along it. They were a quarter of an inch in diameter. Reuben kicked the fence, and several of the poles broke free, hitting the ground with a clang. He took one, pushed the tip against the ground, and bent it with his applied pressure. The end formed a small hook.

The others reached them as he fed the hook into the hole in the metal disc and pulled, dragging the heavy plate free.

Hicks shook her head and stepped back. "I'm not going

down there. Bad enough that we're running, and now you want us to crawl through the old sewers like rats?"

This time Reuben took the lead, climbing down the column of thick damp rungs built into the wall. The metal as rough with corrosion as everything else in this decaying city.

"You're a fucking coward, rookie."

The drones and the blue army were getting closer.

Danko followed Reuben. Groves next.

Hernandez paused at the top. "Shall I pull the cover across, Hicks, or are you coming?"

Hicks' tut went off with a crack. She shook her head. "Fucking cowards." She followed them into the sewers, heaving the steel plate back into place behind her. The light vanished with a heavy *thunk!*

CHAPTER 14

The chains on Fury's gates sang. It had already become a trigger for Reuben's anxiety, but in that moment, the metal whine brought a wave of relief that slightly unclenched the knot in his stomach. The enormous steel doors shook as they opened into the community, welcoming Danko and his team back from another shift.

When the gap in the gates grew wide enough, Sarge strode into view. His hands clasped behind his back again. His voice a thunderclap of authority and accusation. "Where have you been?"

Hicks spat her reply. "We hid like cowards."

Sarge hugged Danko and then pulled back while holding the tops of his arms. He lowered his head, forcing eye contact. His tone softened to the voice he reserved for his most special of recruits. "Are you okay?"

"We hid like cowards," Hicks said again.

Sarge tutted and turned on her. His ruddy cheeks glowed. His glare burned. "You're alive, aren't you?"

Hicks shrugged.

"So I'm guessing Danko made the correct choice?"

Small wrinkles spread away from Hicks' tightened lips.

Sarge put his arm around Danko, but continued to glare at Hicks. "You need to learn to speak when spoken to. Unless you're the leader now?"

Hicks spent more time with her face puce than not. Always fuming about something. Her jaw tight, she trembled as if her self-restraint would falter. As if her venomous retort would flood out of her.

The pause lasted long enough for Hicks to reply. Long enough for Reuben to shift his weight from one foot to the other as if he could shuffle free from the uncomfortable silence. When the vicious woman offered no retort, Sarge shook his head again and returned his focus to Danko.

The bravado that had oozed from Danko when Reuben first met him had now vanished. His actions might be misguided, and he might have a penchant for torture, but, unlike Hicks, he had a heart. "We got chased by Fear's soldiers. There were one hundred of them, at least. Groves got us out of a tight spot. When we were far enough away, we hid. It was hide or die. Were it not for Reuben showing us somewhere safe, we wouldn't be here now."

The sudden attention from Sarge straightened Reuben's back. He nodded at the man. His face burned. He should tell them Groves had found the drain cover.

But Sarge's interest dwindled fast, and he returned his focus to Danko. "But you're all right?"

A damp weight in his chest, Reuben walked on. He followed Hicks' path through Fury's gates. Danko and Sarge fell into a conversation, and Sarge hugged their leader again.

Hernandez caught up to Reuben and pulled him back. Her strength combined with Reuben's fatigue spun him like a weathervane. "You saved my life," she said.

It had been Groves' idea to head into the sewers. She'd found the drain cover. Groves passed between him and

Hernandez. She avoided eye contact. He should have credited her.

"You saved my life twice," Hernandez said, loud enough for Groves to hear. But Groves still didn't look back.

"I was too short to jump, and the rest of them would have left me to fend for myself."

If Groves had seen Hernandez's predicament, she would have helped. She would have jumped back down to make sure they left no one behind.

"And the sewers …" Hernandez said. "Whatever Hicks says, that was a stroke of genius. Well done, Reuben, and thank you."

A polite smile, Reuben said, "Uh … you're welcome." Groves rounded the corner out of sight. What had he done? He stepped away from Hernandez. "I'll … uh … I'll see you tomorrow, yeah?"

Hernandez said something Reuben didn't hear, his focus on Groves. He had to speak to her before she went home. Clear the air. He shouldn't have taken the credit for her plan. What a coward.

His shoulders slumped when he rounded the corner. She'd already gone. The exhaustion from their day finally caught up with him, and his tired legs thrummed. He shook his head. Whatever anyone else thought of his actions today, to the one person who mattered, he'd screwed up. He'd taken all the credit for her ingenuity. What a snake!

CHAPTER 15

"I didn't mean to take the credit, Mum." Reuben sat on the wooden stool in his kitchen. He'd sat on that stool as a little boy. Often when he came home from school and chatted to his mum as she made them both dinner. He sipped from a steaming mug of peppermint tea. Her mug. The rainbow painted around the inside of it now barely visible, years of use causing it to fade like his memories. Like the sound of her voice. The warmth of her touch. The smell of her skin. Or maybe they hadn't faded. Maybe he just thought they had, and if he ever smelled them again, they'd be instant triggers. But he'd never smell them again.

The tulips in the vase didn't have long left, their heads bowed over the edge as if they felt the shame of his error with Groves. "She stopped on the drain cover. I just verbalised her plan. But they thought it was mine. I hadn't even considered I'd be given the credit until they told Sarge, and by then it was already too late." He wrapped his hands around the mug, his palms tingling with the heat. "But it wasn't too late, was it? I should have said something then. Oh, Mum, she must think I'm such a snake."

Reuben slurped his hot drink. Too hot. His lips tingled. "What do you th—"

The knock on the door stopped him dead. Past eight in the evening. The dinner-plate-sized clock on the kitchen wall ticked. It filled the silence. Had he imagined it? Who came out in the city this late? People rarely knocked on his door at the best of times.

Another knock. Three hard raps. Official. Authoritative.

He stood up, the legs of his wooden stool scraping on the stone floor. Movement outside. A silhouette through the glazed window. "W-who is it?" Too short to be Hicks. And not her style. She'd slip a match through the letterbox while he slept if she wanted to get him. Or she'd shove him towards a diseased when they were outside the walls. However she did it, it wouldn't start with the formal gesture of knocking on the door.

The silhouette shifted again, moving their weight from one foot to the other.

Reuben closed one eye and peered through the peephole. His heart leaped and he lost his breath. He stepped back several paces. Look at the state of his house! The plate on the worktop from where he'd finished his dinner and left it. He hadn't cleaned up for the past few days. Dirty clothes on the floor. His bed unmade. And why had she come here? Today of all days. But at least he could get it over and done with in private. Face her wrath today so they could move on tomorrow.

No time to clean. A layer of sweat turned his palms damp. Reuben grabbed the metal door handle. It rattled as an extension of his jitters. If he didn't open it now, she'd never come back.

Reuben opened the door and addressed her feet. "I'm really sorry. I didn't mean to take the credit for your idea. It just came out. I said it, and when they kept heaping praise on me, I felt less and less like I could tell them the truth. By that point, I was going to look like an arsehole in front of someone. I made the wrong choice. I should have looked like an arsehole in front of them, but I feared what Sarge would say. I should have been braver. I should have put them straight. It all happened so fast. I've gone over it a million times already. I wish I could have said it was your idea in the first place. I'll make it right tomorrow. I'll tell everyone the truth. I don't want to take the credit for your ideas. It was you who got us out of that mess. When Danko first introduced you, he'd called you the brains of the group. He was right. I'm sorry."

Groves had stood in silence the entire time. When Reuben finally looked up, he found her smiling at him. "Don't you dare tell them anything!"

"Huh?"

"Taking the credit for the drain cover means you also bore the brunt of Hicks' bullshit about us choosing that route. She wasn't on board with the plan, and she took it out on you. You could have told her it was my idea then, but you protected me. It should be me apologising to you. I don't give a damn about being a hero or being exalted by the others. I just want to do my job. I want to be a cog in the vast military machine. Turn when needed, and rest when not. Otherwise, unremarkable."

"You're far from unremarkable."

"What I'm saying is you can keep the credit."

What started as a slight smile spread into something wider. Reuben batted the air with a limp hand. "Ah, Hicks can do one for all I care. Although, if I'm being honest, I was kind of hoping Sarge might acknowledge me. Whether I deserved it or not."

"Danko's Sarge's golden boy. You shouldn't chase his praise. I fear it will be a lost pursuit."

"So, if you're not pissed with me, why did you storm off when we came back through the gates earlier?"

Groves shook her head. "I didn't. We'd been out much longer than planned, and I needed to get back to Dad and Annabelle." She shrugged before looking over one shoulder and then the other. "Are you going to leave me standing out here all night?"

"Sorry!" Reuben stood aside and pulled the door wider. Before Groves entered, he ran to his bed and quickly made it. He kicked his dirty clothes beneath his armchair. He dropped his dinner plate in the sink with a clatter. "The place is a mess. Sorry."

"We've had a busy few days. You need to rest when you come home, not clean."

He tipped his mint tea away, turning the mug upside down to hide the faded rainbow print inside. He closed a cupboard door, put the bread in the bread bin, and swept the crumbs from the side and caught them. After throwing them in the sink, he rubbed his hands together to clear what remained on his palms, and exhaled. "You're out late."

"We're in the military, Reuben. We can go out when we want."

"That's going to take a bit of getting used to." The silence hung between them before he said, "So … does Annabelle have any nicknames for you?"

"Wha …?"

"I don't have a sibling. I find it funny listening to what they call one another."

Groves shrugged. "Just sis."

"Oh. And your dad?"

"He calls me *mate*. I know what you're doing."

"I don't know what you mean." While folding a tea towel and hanging it on the towel rail, Reuben smiled.

"Who's that?" Groves pointed at the shrine to his mum.

It halted Reuben's momentum. His smile fell, and he coughed to clear his throat. "That's my mum."

"She's …"

"Dead," Reuben said.

"Like my mum."

His eyes itched with the start of tears. He looked at the floor. It had been weeks since he'd last mopped.

"You didn't tell me," Groves said.

Reuben leaned against the worktop. "You didn't ask."

"And your dad?"

"He's alive, but I don't have a relationship with him."

"One of those absent fathers?"

"You could say that."

"What an arsehole."

"He's busy."

"We're all busy. That's no excuse."

Another cough to clear his throat, Reuben took some of his clean plates from the draining board and put them in the cupboard.

"So you live here all alone?"

"I have since I was eleven."

The silence swelled between them. A balloon filling with air. Before it grew too big, Groves put a pin to it with her words. "I also wanted to say good job today."

"Huh?"

"With that couple Danko had his eye on."

"You noticed that?"

"The shiny blade to help them see us? Yeah, of course I did. Good job Hicks didn't work it out, eh? She's itching for an excuse to tear into you."

"Hicks is an arsehole."

"You can say that again."

"Don't worry, I will. So …" Just the thought of saying it

increased Reuben's temperature and quickened his pulse. "That date?"

"Oh." Groves cocked her head to the side and pointed at her chest. "You know my name now? I must have missed that one."

"Mate?"

"Ha!"

A tight press of his lips, Reuben dropped his focus to his dirty floor again.

"G'night, Reuben. See you in the morning. And thanks again. You saved two innocent people, and by telling everyone about the drain cover, you saved our lives and bore the brunt of Hicks' bullshit." She leaned forward and kissed him on his cheek. "See you tomorrow."

Reuben's blush set fire to his face. Sweat lifted beneath his collar. "Uh ... I ... uh ..."

Groves left and closed the door behind her.

His fingers on his cheek where she'd kissed him. The warmth of her contact remained. It would fade like his mother's scent, the sound of her voice, the rainbow pattern on the inside of her mug. But that didn't make it any less real. It had happened. He'd felt it and lived it, regardless of how vivid his memories. Reuben stared through the glazed window. Groves' silhouette merged into the evening as she vanished from sight.

CHAPTER 16

Reuben arrived early for his afternoon shift, closing in on the gates at a jog. Less than half the soldiers had gotten there before him. He slowed to a walk as he joined Danko's line, Hernandez and their leader already waiting. He'd been to see Malcolm to give him his lunch. Give him his lunch, and maybe talk to him about Groves. Seeing as he was already there, it made sense to mention her. Malcolm shared his excitement for the new woman in his life. A genuine friend.

On his way over to the gates, a family had shoved their two children towards him. A boy and girl about four and six years old. They trotted out the obligatory *thank you for your service.* Only a few shifts in and the gesture had already become hollow. But he took it with grace and pushed the image of Hicks to the back of his mind. Of Danko and his mental instability. If they knew what service looked like for some ... He ruffled their heads and moved on. Why shatter the illusion? Hopefully, they'd have the good sense to pick another career.

Even with all the nonsense from Hicks the previous day,

Reuben moved with a lightness of foot he hadn't yet brought to the front gates. He smiled at Hernandez when she looked his way.

She raised her eyebrows. "Someone had a good night last night, then?"

Danko leaned around Hernandez. "Something you're not telling us, new boy?"

Reuben continued to smile. "I had a good night's sleep last night. That's all."

"That's funny. From the way you're grinning, you look like someone who's been up all night. That maybe you've been enjoying your new status as a soldier." Danko left it at that. No snark. No cutting remark. And one noticeable absentee whispering into his ear.

Reuben's heart rate trebled when Groves arrived a few minutes later. His breaths shortened and his cheeks warmed. His voice came out as a high-pitched squeak. "Afternoon." He coughed to clear his throat and lowered his voice. "Afternoon, Groves."

She smiled at him. "Morning, Reuben."

Hernandez stood on tiptoes to make herself visible over Groves' shoulder and winked. Thankfully, Danko had gone to talk with Sarge.

Hicks' arrival shortly after Groves threw a damp blanket over their mood. Her tense frame, her hard scowl. Volatile and ready to erupt given half a chance. Hell, she'd welcome the excuse to lose her shit. She'd actively seek it out. All three of them avoided her eye.

∽

ALL THE UNITS were lined up and ready. Just three dogs going out today. They stood slightly ahead of the teams.

Sarge paced up and down in front of them. Hands behind

his back, as always. His measured steps played their familiar metronomic tap against the asphalt. A man of routine. "This afternoon, I want you all to check the traps. We haven't caught one of Fear's soldiers in a few days. I'm hoping you'll tell me something different when you get back."

"Traps?" Reuben said.

Hicks glared at him.

When she returned her attention to the front, Groves reached back and touched the top of his right arm. "You'll see."

~

After they'd left the city, the rain came down so hard it stung. Storm clouds darkened the sky. Reuben hunched against the frigid assault, his neck sore, his back tight. He'd not yet visited this part of town. The streets were narrow and the old shops packed close together. Or what remained of the old shops. Many of the buildings had partly collapsed. Rubble had spilled into the streets like the entrails of a slit stomach.

Hernandez had to shout over the slamming rain. "This was the poorer side of town. But it's easier for us to move through here with stealth because all the buildings are closer together." Her eyes pinched and her shoulders lifted. She smiled and shrugged. "It might not be pleasurable, but this weather helps mask our steps too. Even the diseased will struggle to place us with so much extra noise."

Around the next corner, they came to a building that stood out for being considerably older than the rest. Made from grey stones of varying sizes and shapes, it came from a time well before many of the decrepit structures that made up its surroundings. It stood in defiance of its derelict environment. The rain bounced off its wonky tiled roof. One of the few buildings that still had a roof. "What's that place?" Reuben said.

"It used to be a public house." Hernandez continued to be his tour guide, keeping her voice low enough to avoid Hicks' involvement. "It was somewhere people would go to get inebriated, back in the day when alcohol was legal." She snorted a laugh and shook her head.

"What?" Reuben said.

"Just imagine it! Imagine what Fury would be like if they let people drink. I'm so—"

Danko dropped into a hunch. Hicks raised her baton.

At first Reuben had mistaken it for a sinkhole. At least twenty feet long and six to eight feet wide. But the sides were too straight. This pit had been intentionally created. A blonde girl of about fourteen hung over the edge. Her upper body lay on the damp road, her legs hanging into the hole. She wore Fear's blue uniform. Reuben leaned closer to Hernandez. "How young do they enlist them in Fear?"

"If they think they're ready, and by ready, I mean able to hold a baton and swing it, then they enlist them."

"They don't have a choice?"

Hernandez shook her head.

"She's just a baby."

Hicks remained focused on the girl, but stepped back a pace to be closer to Reuben and Hernandez. She spoke from the side of her mouth. "A baby who chose the wrong day to get caught." The frown she'd brought to their shift had now gone, replaced by a sadistic smile. She approached the girl, flashed her small teeth at the young soldier, and held a hand in her direction. Her sickly-sweet tone played a chill down Reuben's spine and he shivered. "Let me help you up, sweetie."

The temperature dropped, and the rain came down harder. Even Mother Nature feared for the young girl.

Hicks helped Fear's soldier to her feet.

Skinny and wretched in her sodden clothes, the girl stood with her right foot raised on tiptoes and her right arm hanging limp at her side.

"It's quite a fall, eh?" Hicks said.

The girl's childish features buckled. Her bottom lip turned down. She quivered as she nodded. Her blonde hair, dark with damp, clung to her face.

"What's wrong?" Hicks said.

The girl shook her head.

Hicks put an arm around her, pulling her tight, crushing her already broken right side.

The girl whimpered.

"You don't need to be frightened of us." Hicks' tone was so smooth Reuben almost fell for it. He caught himself leaning towards her as if sucked in by an invisible force. "We're all friends in this city."

The girl turned away with a sharp twist and broke into a hobbling run.

Hicks laughed, giving the girl a lead of about ten feet before she darted after the wounded creature. One sweep and she cleared the girl's legs from beneath her, kicking her so hard the girl's feet lifted to shoulder height before she came down again.

The girl screamed when she landed on her right side. She rolled on the floor in the rain. "Please!" The girl flipped over onto her back, her feet slipping on the road from where she pushed herself away from Hicks. "I was on my first run, and I fell into that trap."

Reuben walked with Groves and Hernandez, who followed Hicks and the girl. They passed the pit, the drop at least thirty feet to a ground covered in rubble. Sheer walls with no apparent hand- or footholds. "How the hell did she survive that fall?"

"And then climb out of there?" Hernandez said.

"If you let me go," the girl said, "I won't go back to Fear. I'll leave this city and never return. You won't have to worry about me."

"Oh, sweetie." Hicks shook her head, Danko now at her side. "It doesn't work like that. You see, if one of your lot catches one of our lot, well ..." Hicks spread her arms wide, palms to the sky. "Do you know what they'd do to us?"

The girl sobbed.

Reuben scanned their surroundings. Not that he wanted to see them, but if a small horde arrived now, it might give the girl a chance to get away.

"So you understand the situation we're in? Besides ..." Hicks' cheery demeanour dropped like a rookie falling into a pit. Thunder rolled beneath her words. "I fucking *hate* rookies." She cast a glance back.

Reuben balled his fists. He could catch her unawares and throw her into the pit right now.

"But, you know ... on second thoughts."

The girl raised her head.

"Who am I kidding?" Hicks took a two-step run-up and kicked the side of her face. The *crack* of her boot connecting boomeranged off the walls surrounding them. She pulled Fury's flag from her back pocket, snapping it open in the strong wind before handing it to Danko.

Groves and Hernandez stepped back, and both of them turned the other way.

"Come on," Reuben said, "do you really need to be so harsh?"

"She's the enemy, *rookie!*"

"I get that, Hicks, and I get that we need to kill her, but there are a million different ways to kill someone."

"And how I'd like to try every one of them out on you.

Besides, *new boy*, what do you think they'd do to us? Jeez, You're so fucking naïve."

"Danko," Reuben said, "if Fear's army is going to do to us what Hicks says they will."

"There's no *if* about it," Hicks said.

"Then it makes no difference what we do now. We could just end her. Make it quick and simple. And you know what, that compassion might inspire them to do the same to one of ours when they catch us. From what Hicks says, it can't get any worse. Maybe it's time to try something new?"

"Will you listen to him?" Hicks pointed at Reuben. "He's so green he's almost plant life. Although, I wouldn't mind betting a lot of plant life is more dangerous than him. Are you really going to take anything this sapling says seriously? If you show Fear's army you're going soft, they'll take advantage. They'll think they've won."

"Come on, Danko," Reuben said, "you know it makes sense."

Hicks' voice grew louder, and her words gathered momentum. "What will Sarge say when he finds out you went easy on the enemy? That you felt any level of empathy for one of Fear's soldiers?"

"He'll think he's human," Reuben said.

Hicks sneered at him. "You have a lot to learn about Sarge."

His knife in one hand, Fury's flag in the other, his shoulders slumped, and his eyes already glazed with remorse, Danko mounted Fear's flaccid rookie like he had the diseased, sitting on her chest and kneeling on her shoulders, pinning her to the ground beneath his weight.

"Danko," Reuben said.

The first time Reuben had seen Hicks' knife. Its tip now hovered an inch from his left eyeball. "Give me one excuse, rookie. Go on, I dare ya."

Reuben drew a breath to settle his heart and held Hicks' glare. The hammering rain filled the silence, the occasional drop bursting on the knife and splashing his face.

"Now come on, Danko," Hicks said, pulling her blade away. "Remember what they did to Smith."

His knife in his left hand, Danko gathered Fury's flag in his right fist.

Hicks stepped closer. "And Wellington. And Scout. And Parker. And Wellbelove. And Bond."

Each name added to Danko's already violent shake.

"And don't forget Anita Swan."

"Yeargh!" Danko threw his entire bodyweight into the blow. His right fist, the flag poking from the sides, slammed into the centre of the fourteen-year-old's delicate face.

One blow turned the girl's nose into a bloody pulp. She gasped, her mouth wide.

Danko moved fast. He'd done this a thousand times before. Gagging her with Fury's flag, he then used two thick fingers to push the red fabric deep into the girl's throat, pulling them out before she bit him.

Reuben stepped forwards. "What the hell, Danko?" The girl's face had turned puce, and her eyes bulged.

Danko ripped the flag from the girl's mouth and turned on Reuben. Tears mixed with the rainwater soaking his face. He pointed his knife at him. "You're on very fucking thin ice, new boy. Wind your neck in before I tear a ragged gash in it and leave you to bleed out on the road."

Reuben stepped back to be with Hernandez and Groves. The slightest contact from where she touched the base of his back, Groves said, "You did all you could."

"You only need one eye to see this." Danko's left hand shook as he pressed the tip of the knife into the girl's right eye.

The girl screamed, kicked, and bucked, but she had no

chance against Danko's weight. Tears of blood ran down the side of her face. She cried like a diseased.

"That's it," Hicks said, bouncing on the spot, her face alive. "Make the bitch pay."

Reuben shook his head and walked away.

"Where are you going, rookie?"

"I can't watch this."

"You're ignoring your duty?" Hicks said.

"I want to fight for this city. I believe in the cause, and I accept I'll have to kill Fear's soldiers." Reuben shook his head. "But not like this. This isn't who I am, and this isn't what the people of Fury demand. This isn't what I signed up for."

"Maybe you're no soldier, then."

"Maybe I'm not the one who's confused about the role of a soldier."

Hicks charged Reuben. But before she reached him, Hernandez stepped between them. She shoved her back, Hicks stumbling, her arms flapping to maintain her balance. The two women stared at one another. Bodies wound tight, fists balled. Hernandez might have been a foot shorter, but she had biceps like cannonballs. "You've gone too far, Hicks. You need to back off and calm the fuck down."

Hicks' green eyes narrowed before she turned around and walked back to Danko's side. She leaned over his shoulder while he used his knife to remove the young girl's ear.

CHAPTER 17

The same pose Sarge always adopted. Hands behind his back and a deep scowl on his weathered face. He marched a few steps out into the city like one of Reuben's old wind-up toys and waited while Danko led his team back from another shift. "You look like you've had another encounter." His mouth twitched towards a smile. "Another diseased?"

Reuben's heart beat harder when Danko didn't reply. No one ignored Sarge.

"He was amazing, Sarge."

Fixing on Hicks, Sarge looked from Danko to her and back to Danko as if weighing up his options. Did he let Danko get away with such blatant disrespect?

"I think he's just recovering, sir. Finding his way again after going to town on one of Fear's soldiers. He sent them a message. It was a good job, but, I must say, it was also a lot for one person to endure. On both sides, Danko and his victim."

"And …" Sarge's predatory gaze narrowed on Danko. Did

he let it slide? Back to Hicks, a slight loosening of his taut frame. "Did you leave a flag?"

"Yes, sir." Hicks nodded. "He used mine. Damn near choked the bitch on it and then left it with her mutilated corpse. No room for ambiguity when Fear find her."

Mirth ironed out the wrinkles on Sarge's face. "That's what I like to hear."

Reuben's stomach churned. Maybe Sarge only backed up Danko's actions because he hadn't witnessed them. Would he have encouraged what had happened had he been there? Could he have stood by? Had he done far worse himself when he went outside the city?

"So what happened?" Sarge said. "Give me the details."

Like Sarge, Hicks had come alive because of Danko's actions. "The enemy was trying to get away. She fell into one of our pits. By the time we'd reached her, she'd almost climbed all the way out. So Danko made a proper example of her. We only hope that Fear find her before the scavengers."

"Did she put up a fight?"

Hicks shook her head. "We didn't give her a chance."

"Good."

"She was just a kid," Reuben said. Groves gasped and Hicks turned on him, snapping around so fast he barely saw her move. But screw her. He had to say this. "The *soldier* can't have been any older than fourteen. At the most. She stood no chance against a fully grown man like Danko. He pinned her down and slowly cut her to shreds. There was no honour in what just happened."

Sarge knocked Groves aside as he made a beeline for Reuben. "Are you saying we should have gone easy on her? Let her live?

Malcolm's words rang through his head. Don't lose track of who he is. Easier said than done when staring down the barrels of Sarge's fury. A shake of his head,

Reuben said, "No. Not at all." He lowered his gaze and twisted away from their enraged leader. His sodden uniform clung to him. "I'm just questioning the choice to cut her to shreds." His voice wobbled. "We were always going to kill her. Surely that sends enough of a message? Why then burst her eyeball, cut her ears and nose off, tear her torso wide open, and ..." He sighed. "We could have done all that to her corpse if we'd wanted to send a message. How can we walk through the streets of this city with our heads held high if this is what we do to minors? What do you reckon the people of Fury would think of us if they saw that? How many of them would thank us for our service if they found out what *really* happened outside the walls?"

"The enemy takes many forms," Sarge said. "A tiger's fur might be pleasant to stroke, but the animal will still bite your head off when it gets hungry. And Fear are hungry. In fact, they're ravenous."

"I didn't say we shouldn't kill her."

Sarge's features hardened. "I've given you a chance to speak. Now shut the fuck up."

Hicks walked around Sarge and grabbed Reuben by his shirt. "Go home, rookie, before you talk yourself into some serious trouble." She dragged him away from the group and shoved him towards the city. "And don't think I've let this slide."

Several stumbling steps, Reuben turned around and faced Sarge again, shivering from the damp press of his uniform.

"Are you deaf or something?" Sarge said. "You'd do well to listen to her. I've only got so much patience, and I've already reached my limit."

Hernandez and Groves walked back into the city side by side. Groves shook her head at Reuben. Condemnation? Friendly advice? Either way, it didn't matter. He couldn't lose himself while doing this work. If he gave up his morals, then what remained? Why bother? He held his ground.

Sarge closed the gap between them and cuffed Reuben around the side of the head. The crack of his thick hand felt like being hit with a wooden club. Reuben's ears rang.

Hatred replaced Sarge's stoicism. He gritted his yellow teeth. Spittle flew from his mouth when he said, "Fuck off, rookie. Learn when it's your turn to speak, and learn when to shut the fuck up. If you don't get away from me, I *will* make an example of you. What just happened to that girl will be a breeze compared to what we'll do to you."

"Besides," Hicks said, "we're back on shift in a few hours. Go home and get the rest you need. You're tired, and it's been a stressful day. I'm sure you don't know what you're saying right now. The ice beneath your feet might be wafer thin, but it's yet to give out. Remember that when you take your next step."

A thousand responses raced to the end of Reuben's tongue. Each of them a rational and justified point. Each of them needing to be said. Was this who they were? Was this something to be proud of? But he had the wrong audience. No matter how much reason and logic he brought to the argument, they wouldn't hear it.

Sarge balled his gigantic hands into fists.

Reuben finally took the hint and left.

CHAPTER 18

The woman turned Reuben's stomach at the best of times, so when Hicks chowed down on the charred canid, his throat damn near turned inside out as he fought to suppress his heave. She threw her head back and flung her mouth wide with a belly laugh. Half-chewed fox lay on her tongue, and her maw glistened with grease. Several yellow-tinged drops had collected on her chin, and a small chunk of meat clung to her bottom lip. Reuben stared at it when she pointed at him and said, "That one's soft in the head."

There were twenty-two of them in the basement car park of the old hotel. Concrete walls and floor, the place clung onto the damp from the rain of a few hours previously. His front warmed by the fire, his bottom numbed from the cold ground. The smoke tightened his lungs and stung his tired eyes. No amount of blinking relieved the discomfort. Another unit had caught the fox. A spit driven through it, a soldier Reuben didn't know turned it over the flames. Although plenty of cooked meat remained, they'd taken the best cuts, and much of what they'd left needed to be chewed from the bone. Not that he'd eat tonight. He'd have to spend more time living this life before he came anywhere close to developing an appetite while on the job.

Hicks' obnoxious voice echoed in the underground space. Gone one in the morning, it ran from the car park and called out into the still city to anyone who cared to hear. Maybe she did it to invite conflict. Diseased or soldiers, she didn't care. The woman thrived on chaos and held no regard for which way the odds were stacked. "He tried to rat out me and Danko to Sarge."

"I didn't!" Reuben shook his head. "I just challenged your methods. Sarge's methods. I wasn't ratting out anyone. I just think there's another way."

The chunk of fox fell from Hicks' lip when she leaned closer to him. The fire's flickering light played with the shadows on her face. "If we don't get them first and hit them hard, they'll see us as weak. They'll destroy us. The other ways you want to explore will end up with us *dead*."

"You should try it sometime," one of the other leaders said. A man in his mid to late twenties, he had tanned skin and his hair shaved to his scalp. On each cheek, he had three parallel scars, each line about an inch and a half long. They were self-inflicted and stained black. He remained fixed on Reuben, daring him to reply. The fire between them crackled and popped.

Groves threw Reuben the occasional glance, but she dropped her gaze when he looked back. Hernandez sat away from the fire, leaning against a wall and picking her nails. Danko ate in silence while Hicks grinned like a moron at his side, blissfully ignorant to the true cost of what had happened the last time they were out. He carried the burden of what he'd done to the girl in his hunched frame. A trauma to add to the many before it. A burden he'd take to the grave.

"The thing is—" Hicks snorted as she laughed "—the

rookie thought Sarge would be on his side. That he'd agree about us going easier on Fear's army."

"Are you soft in the head, rookie?" Of all the people there, the scarred and bald team leader seemed to have the tightest bond with Hicks. They obviously shared similar philosophies.

"I think he's simple," Hicks said.

"He's learning." Hernandez leaned away from the wall. "We all needed to at some point. Go easy on him, yeah?"

Hicks snarled, but another soldier from a different unit spoke before she could, "We all made mistakes when we started." Among the oldest soldiers there, she was in her mid to late thirties. She raised her eyebrows. "Even you, Hicks. Allow the boy the time he needs to learn."

"Not if his mistakes cost me my life." Hicks dragged her sleeve across her chin. The grease stains turned the crimson fabric darker. "He has to learn fast. And putting Sarge's nose out of joint ain't the way to go. Even I knew that as a rookie."

Crack! A door behind them burst open. It cut through the conversation and snapped all twenty-two of them alert. Reuben reached back for Groves, touching her leg before he pulled away. She could look after herself. He should focus on him.

Seven civilians spilled into the car park, one after the other. All of them were in their late teens to early twenties. Four of them female, three male. They were all out of breath and sweating, gasping from what must have been a chase.

The leader with the scarred cheeks stood up and waved his baton at them. He approached them with measured steps. His head snapped to one side. "Well, well, what have we here, then?"

"Uh ..." The girl who spoke appeared to be the group's leader. She had long ginger hair in a plait that rested between her shoulder blades. "We ... uh—"

"Shut the fuck up!" The leader with the baton stepped closer. The others had gotten to their feet and fanned out behind him. A pack of predators, they shimmered with restraint. Say the word and they'd tear this lot to shreds. He pointed his baton at the main girl and showed her where he wanted them to go with a flick of his weapon. He guided them away from the door into the middle of the car park.

What were they about to do to these people? Reuben kept his baton lowered. He might have no control over their actions, but he didn't have to play a part. Be true to who he is. He didn't kill innocent people. And if he took a life in battle, he'd kill them quick and clean.

"What do you want with us?" the ginger girl said.

The leader with the scars moved fast, crashing into her and slamming her up against a wall. He pressed his forearm to her throat, the girl's pale skin turning puce.

Hicks spread her arms wide to hold the others back. All the while, Danko remained sat by the fire. The only one who hadn't moved, he fixed on the shimmering orange flames with glazed eyes.

The scarred soldier spoke with a low voice. His words rumbled. "We've not decided yet." He pressed his crotch into her. "But I promise you it will be worse if you don't shut the fuck up."

Hicks pointed her baton at Reuben and then Groves. "You two! Monitor them while we finish our meal. We have time, so we need to decide the best way to fuck these people up, and who gets the honour of doing it. I'm wondering if it might be time for the rookie to pop his cherry."

It took the scarred leader a little longer than the others to return to the fire. He carried his disappointment in his stooped frame. Hicks hadn't needed to say it, but even she had a line. As if holding onto some of his pride, he kept the ginger girl fixed with his ravenous gaze. The girl returned his stare with interest. Let him try. See what happens to him when he does. She'd go down fighting, and she'd make sure he fell with her. Had Reuben picked the wrong side?

Maybe Groves knew Reuben well enough, or maybe his face said it all. She spoke to him in a whisper. "If you let them go, they will do to you what they have planned for them. Even that psycho with the scars."

Reuben shuddered.

"You need to learn when you can influence a situation, because this isn't one of those times."

The shortest of the hostages, a small young woman, her eyes white-hot with rage, focused on Reuben. "You think you're going to win this one, don't you? I can tell you now, you're seriously mistaken. Let us go and we'll be on our way. Take this any further, and I promise you, you'll regret it."

The slap of tired footsteps entered the car park via the ramp from the street. A young man in his teens. Young, but clearly fit. Dressed in civilian clothes like the others, his wide chest rose and fell with his breaths. His jaw hung loose.

The soldier with the scars moved as if to challenge the boy. But he stopped.

Reuben frowned. "Why's he not—"

Before he could finish the sentence, the air thrummed with the collective hum of drones.

Groves said, "Oh fuck!"

CHAPTER 19

"Drones!"
The girl hadn't needed to say it. A rookie like Reuben, she belonged to the unit closest to the underground car park's exit ramp. Closest to the boy who'd ushered in their hovering executors. The rookie's scream joined the drones' hum, which grew louder as the first of the machines entered the enclosed underground space. Two more came in behind. Large mechanical bugs with Gatling gun arms and spotlights for noses. Their weapons spun, whirring with their shrill battle cry. Their pied piper ran one way while the drones turned the other. They now only had sensors for their true enemy, zeroing in on the rookie who'd announced their arrival. A high-pitched whine met her wild scream. The Gatling guns released their stuttered assault. Bursts of red mist like damp fireworks from where the bullets tore into her soft flesh.

The girl snapped, jolted, and eventually fell limp. Hicks sneered. "Well, at least that shut her up."

Groves' grip stung Reuben's right arm when she latched onto him and pulled him behind a stone pillar.

The steel door that had let their prisoners into the car park now let them back out again. It crashed against the wall from where they threw it wide, and the group vanished back up the stairs, the newest arrival taking up the rear.

Screams joined the echo of bullet fire. More drones entered the car park. Their bullets scythed down soldiers. Limbs snapped and bodies spasmed. Hicks shook from the effort it took to deliver her order. "Follow me if you want to survive this."

While the soldiers closest to the drones fell, Hicks took them down to the next level of the car park. Their closest escape route.

The ramp dropped into a sharp decline that accelerated their escape. Reuben fought against his tight lungs from his past hour in front of the smoking fire. He called ahead, "Can we even get out this way?"

"You question me once more, rookie," Hicks called back, "and you're on your own. Now shut your fucking mouth and keep up."

The screams above them quietened. The drones had executed the slaughter with cold efficiency. They hummed as if in conversation. Reuben followed Hicks and the others into the darkness. He caught Groves' hand when she reached back to him.

"You all need to hold hands and follow me," Hicks said. "I know how these things work and how best to avoid them. If we can give them the slip, we can get out of here. They lock onto us again, especially now there are no more soldiers to distract them, and we're screwed."

They moved at a fast walk. A wall on their left, Reuben dragged his free hand along the rough surface. If they needed to bolt, at least he'd know which way he couldn't run. Although it still gave him too many options, especially when he couldn't see any of them.

The collective glow of five to ten drones swelled through the car park's next level as they descended the ramp. The bass note hum of their levitation thrummed through the enclosed space. Searchlights accompanied the throbbing tone. They were predators flushing out their prey. They didn't need stealth. They'd already won.

The drones fanned out, casting their net of white light wider. It altered the shadows from the concrete pillars. They grew and shortened like time-lapsed footage of a sundial.

The wall on Reuben's left gave way to air. Now three hundred and sixty degrees of blind options. Groves, as an extension of the line ahead, snapped a sharp tug on his arm, turning him left and encouraging him into a run. Their feet scuffed the ground. But the drones couldn't have heard them. They continued their slow scanning of the underground space.

Groves tugged Reuben again. Another ninety-degree left turn. It snapped through him and stung his shoulder. One hundred feet of running blind and they turned left again. They headed back in the direction they'd come from.

Where the drone's light had been behind them, it now burned as a faint glow ahead. The headlights were facing away from them. The car park, a large circuit, had allowed them to double back on themselves. If they got this right, the drones' slow search would lead them to their inevitable conclusion far too late, and they'd be long gone.

Reuben slammed into Groves when she stopped, shoving her and the other three forwards several steps. They'd halted because one drone remained on the ramp leading out of there.

They grouped together, twenty feet from the hovering bot. Their surroundings were illuminated by the glow of its spotlight. Hicks said, "Fuck it! I was hoping they'd all joined the search party."

Hicks had done nothing but dig out Reuben for being useless. Maybe this moment had come for a reason. Maybe he needed to show her he had much more value than she'd given him credit for. All the while he'd held Groves hand. The only two yet to let go of one another. Were his life not in danger, he would have held on longer. He would have held on for days. When he let go, she turned to him and raised her eyebrows. He dipped her the slightest nod. He had this.

Reuben ran towards the drone at a crouch. His baton in his right hand, he stuck to the shadows. He halved the distance between him and the large metal bug.

He burst from cover with just a few feet to go. The drone turned Reuben's way, its light dazzling him. Its guns whirred.

One chance. Reuben jumped, smashed the lamp on the front of the drone, and then dived beneath it. He crawled under the blinded machine as it twisted and turned, sending out an indiscriminate wave of bullets. Shards and chips of concrete sprayed his back.

Beneath the large metal beast, Reuben swung for one of its guns and knocked it clean away from its body. He smashed the other one before it could aim at him. The vibration from the hard contact stung his tight grip.

The second gun remained attached, but it hung limp and ineffective.

Before Reuben could yell for the others, Hicks charged past him up the ramp. "You fucking moron!"

The flood of lights from the search party of drones had given chase.

Danko ran up the ramp next, Hernandez and Groves level with one another as they made their way to the floor above. They had a few hundred feet lead over the drones at the most. He might have immobilised one bot, but they were still vastly outnumbered and outgunned.

Back on the first floor, the moonlight shone down the

ramps and provided the guidance they needed to get to the street. The silhouettes of the rest of his team headed for the closest exit. Reuben caught his foot and tripped, the obstruction like a damp sand bag. He fell and lost his grip on his baton. It clanged away from him. His palms bore the brunt of his stumble, burning from where the rough concrete bit into them. The moonlight revealed the crimson-uniformed cadaver. Blood pooled beneath it. Deep red bullet holes pockmarked its face. The hum of the drones closed in. He'd be next.

Back up on his weak legs, his lungs tight. Reuben's team had already left. He hit the steep ramp out of there and ran up into the street. The moon illuminated the empty road. Every surface glistened with damp from the earlier downpour. Where had his team gone? They could be in any of the shadows of the surrounding buildings. Each man and woman for themselves. They'd left him. And maybe he deserved it. A first-class liability. What a moron. He cupped his mouth with his hands. "Gro—"

Clack-clack, clack-clack.

They were out in the city with him. But were they close enough?

The car park and the drones at his back. A deep hum, condensed by the underground space, it shot out into the night as a death threat.

Clack-clack, clack-clack.

The drones' lights ran ahead of them, exiting the car park before they did.

Whomp! An orange glow of fire. The first of the dogs burst from the darkness and charged down the illuminated ramp. Its flames met the first drone. Several more of the robotic quadrupeds joined the attack. The lead drone hit the ground with a *clang!* Its charred husk smoked. The dogs swarmed down the Ramp, driving back Fear's bots.

Reuben's pulse pounded. His head spun. Eyes on fire from the smoke, exhaustion, and searching the surrounding shadows for his unit. Wherever they were, he'd do better reuniting with them inside Fury's walls. Waiting here would only get him killed. Hopefully, they were already on their way back. He set off. It might have been a bold move to take down the drone, and Hicks might well be pissed with him, but even someone as miserable as her would have to admit it had worked.

CHAPTER 20

Another deep whoosh lit several of the underground car park's exits with an orange glow. The tall and tatty hotel, windowless, derelict, and ragged, stood like a monument to the underworld. The space beneath it was aglow with fire and brimstone, the drones and dogs locked in battle. Despite being forty feet from the closest ramp, Reuben stumbled back from the wall of heat. His skin itched with sweat. The stuttered gunfire responded to the roaring flames. The clacking of the dogs. The drones' whir. The conversation of war between the two sides' fiercest soldiers. But which side would win today? If the drones emerged, they'd best not find him there gawking like an idiot. He took off into the night.

Now several streets away. Far enough to make him safe. For now. Reuben slowed to a walk, his surroundings made up of broken and decrepit towers, abandoned shops, houses that rested against one another as if their structural integrity relied on the support of their neighbours. How the hell would he find his way back to Fury? He'd left the city a handful of times in the past few days. He didn't know his way around. And the areas he might have visited during the day looked different at night.

The moon's silver glow got dissected by the towers. Shadows lurked inside every building, down every alley, and pressed up against walls. Did anyone watch him at that moment? The furore beneath the hotel must have alerted Fear's army. What about the diseased?

Reuben's heart slammed against his ribcage as if desperate for release. He snapped his head left and right. Lower his guard for a second and someone would take his back and cut his throat.

The three tallest towers in the city were the only landmark Reuben recognised. Night or day. They stood proud. Going for them had to be better than running without direction or purpose.

The main roads were a straightforward route to travel, but they left him exposed.

"Fuck this!" Reuben turned off the main road and jumped through the large hole where a window had once fronted an old shop. Pieces of rotten wood lay scattered across the ground. Kicked from the frame, years of entropy had turned it soft. His steps pressed them to dust. The moonlight highlighted the flecks of paint peeling from the grimy walls.

Another check behind, Reuben darted through a small doorway and burst out into an alley. A long and dark walkway, it ran parallel to the main roads on either side. Both the one he'd left behind and the one loaded with landmines.

Closer to the three towers, he now moved through their long shadows. They loomed over him. They fixed him with their judgement. So the rookie had made it this far, but did he know his way home? A lost child in the market. Maybe his only option would be to sit on the ground and cry in the hope an adult could help him find his way. He sneered up at the phallic guardians. "What do you know? I'll get back to Fury. You'll see."

The towers stood in a line. And while they were almost identical, slight differences distinguished each one from its neighbours. He might not have been in the city many times, but he hadn't needed to go beyond the walls to know these structures. They'd watched over him from the day he'd been born. When boredom struck, he'd wish away the hours staring out at the city, dreaming of his future life in the military. He shook his head. The reality had come nowhere near to his fantasy. But, with the spare time of a child, he'd noticed things a busier person might have missed. Like the design around the top of each of the towers.

All three of their pinnacles had a tiled lip. On two of them, the tiles were shaped like diamonds. One had triangles. That one stood the farthest away from Fury.

The scuff of a footstep on his right. Reuben gasped. He spun toward the nearest alley. His hands balled in fists. His baton remained on the floor of the hotel's car park

For the next thirty seconds, the city held its breath with Reuben. The only sound came from the raging battle at the base of the hotel behind him. He continued towards the towers.

The triangle-tiled building on his left, he turned right. "See." He swore at the buildings with two raised fingers. "I'll find my way home from here."

Reuben ducked through another shop, this one filled with the twisted metal that had once been clothes rails. His unblinking eyes stung. He hopped over the small wall that had supported the weight of the shop window, several chunks of glass popping beneath his steps. The shadows continued to observe.

He ran across the main road towards more alleys.

"Hey!"

The accusation struck like lightning and Reuben froze. "Shit!"

"Enemy!" A blue soldier pointed at Reuben.

"Fuck!" How had he missed them?

Fifty feet away, the soldier shouted again. "One of Fury's soldiers. Enemy!"

Reuben vanished into the alley.

The soldier gave chase.

The steps of one multiplied. Reuben's already tired legs weakened. He should just give up now. Curl into a ball and hope they ended him quickly. But he kept moving. The need to survive overrode his faltering courage. He rounded a right-angled bend.

The close alley amplified his pursuers' steps. They were gaining on him.

No time to check, Reuben ran from the next alley, crossed the next main road, and vanished into the darkness again.

Fear's soldiers were faster than him. If he didn't evade them, he'd die.

Reuben turned left down another narrow path instead of heading for the next main road. It led him to a smaller street flanked by rows of shops. All of them had flat roofs. Fire escapes clung to the sides of many. Should he go through them or over? On a roof, they might miss him. It would give him somewhere to hide. Somewhere to hide as long as they didn't know where he'd gone. If they followed him, he'd get cornered.

Reuben jumped into another old shop. He kicked the wooden door at the back from its hinges. A cloud of dust burst from the breaking wood. He dragged in a lungful with his next gasp. His chest twisted, and he coughed several times. He heaved, but the tickle remained deep in his throat.

The white glow from a drone's beam affirmed Reuben's

decision. Had he been on the roofs, the spotlight would have found him in seconds.

Back on another main road. He knew this place! A left turn would lead him to the old shopping centre. Right took him to the labyrinthine residential area. He ran right.

The soldiers might have remained on his tail, the hum of at least one drone behind him too, but the twists and turns of the tight alleys allowed him to stretch his lead. The itch in his throat grew worse. His chest wound tighter. Stars swam in his vision. He had to find somewhere to hide. It might not pay off, but he couldn't run forever.

Reuben entered an old house through the back. He ran down the hallway and out the front door. Fear's army remained on his tail. If he could hear them, chances were they could hear him. He ran into the next derelict house, into one of the reception rooms, and out through a window into the back garden.

A seven-foot wall, Reuben grabbed the top and dragged himself over. His feet slapped down against the path on the other side. Fear's army's steps had grown fainter.

At the next house, Reuben halted in a small dark room. It had a built-in, full-length cupboard in the corner. A shelf sectioned off the top quarter. He dragged himself up and curled in the dark space, pulling the door closed behind him.

Despite his best efforts to get his breathing under control, Reuben panted and gasped. Curled in a ball, it crushed his diaphragm.

Less than a minute passed before the glow from a drone lit up the outside of the house. Shards of light found the gaps in the cupboard's door. Three male voices entered the building. They spoke one after the other.

"Where is he?"

"He's got to be here somewhere."

"Jacobs, you wait here. Sound your whistle if you see him."

A female voice replied, "Yes, sir."

The glow from the drone vanished. The hum of its propellors faded. The soldiers' steps followed. But they'd left Jacobs behind. Reuben could wait it out. They'd give up on him eventually. In a big city like this, he could be anywhere. At some point they'd have to write off the search as futile.

His breaths easing, Reuben sank into the low thrum of fatigue occupying his body. He just had to wait it out.

The shelf creaked.

Apparently, the cupboard he'd used as a hidey-hole had very different ideas. "Oh, fuck!"

The vibration from the splintering wood ran through him. A popping crack like the surface of a thawing lake.

Another creak. This time it ran from one side of the shelf all the way to the other.

He didn't have long before it dropped him like a sack of rocks.

CHAPTER 21

The shelf broke with a crack and tearing of splintering wood. It turned Reuben weightless, throwing his stomach into his throat. He hit the ground with a thud that drove the air from his lungs. It sent a streak up his back that ended as a fiery ball of agony beneath his right shoulder blade.

Barking for air, he rolled away from the cupboard. Footsteps descended on his location. They started outside and came quickly. It sounded like just one person. The woman they'd tasked with watching him?

Reuben scrambled to his feet, holding his back with his right hand. He stabilised himself against the wall with his left.

The tight hallway condensed the sound of her steps. Reuben could meet her head-on. But what threat did he pose? He could barely stand, and he had no baton. Who knew what weapon she carried. It had to be more than a pair of fists and a body that hadn't learned how to throw them. What if she had a drone with her?

A glint of metal caught his eye. One of the poles that had

supported the now fallen shelf. Covered in rust, but it'd do. Until he grabbed it. The thing crumbled in his grip. "Fuck it."

Reuben fell back into the cupboard and covered himself with what remained of the broken wooden shelf. A snivelling creature cowering in the corner. He pulled his knees into his chest and trembled. The heavy pieces of the wooden shelf leaned against him. He drew air in through his nose and let it out through his mouth.

The steps slowed down as the woman entered the room. Reuben's heart hammered. His chest tightened again. He breathed in through his nose and out through his mouth.

Tock. Tock. Tock.

Her steps came closer. She must have been just feet away. Were it not for his own quickened pulse driving his hammering heart, he might have been able to locate her better. Had she already seen him?

In through his nose. Out through his mouth. Cowering behind the sheet of wood. In through his nose. Out through his mouth.

The steps halted. Maybe she stood watching him. Maybe she had her back to him.

Reuben tensed and slowly reached up to feel the back edge of the broken shelf, the wood jagged from where it had snapped. Clamping his top teeth on his bottom lip, he lifted the shelf away.

He froze.

The silhouette of the soldier stood over him.

The tip of their sword hovered a foot from Reuben's face. One lunge would end him.

But it wasn't the woman tasked with watching him. The soldier stood about as tall as Reuben, but his frame had thickened with age. He spoke in a measured tone as if trying to encourage Reuben to remain calm. An attempt to control the situation. "Now move slowly."

His stomach in knots, Reuben's body betrayed him, his hands shaking as he tried to lay the shelf flat. It hit the concrete ground with a gentle slap.

The soldier backed away. "Now come out with your hands up. Or I can come in there and stick you like a wounded pig?"

"No!" Reuben's echo mocked him. A pathetic warble. A febrile plea for mercy. But maybe he should remain in the same spot. Force the soldier to execute him now. It would be much easier than what Hicks had promised would happen. Compared to the fate of many others, dying curled in a ball in a dark corner would be a blessing.

But, once again, his survival instinct kicked in. A tiny shred of hope that everything would be okay. That maybe this time would be different. He used the wall to push against so he could get to his feet. More spasms streaked up his back, stoking the already burning pain beneath his shoulder blade. It gripped his body. Restricted his breaths. Adrenaline flooded his system, and he shook beyond his control.

As Reuben came forward, the soldier stepped back, allowing him the space he needed. The moonlight shone through the window, revealing more of the man than just his silhouette. In his late twenties to early thirties, he'd done some time in the army. He had experience. He knew all the tricks. His thick black hair had been closely cropped, and his brown eyes were soft, almost as if he already felt remorse for Reuben's fate.

"What are you going to do to me?" Reuben said.

Fear's soldier stepped back again, moving closer to the window. He shook his head and sighed. "Would you look at this. A rookie. What, you been on the job a day? A week? Your uniform still has the creases in it. You look like your mum dressed you."

Reuben bit back his reply. He gulped it back down. He

clenched his jaw as if it would somehow ease his trembling. His words warbled. "Yeah, something like that."

"You're probably still believing in the ideal sold to you by the higher-ups. That you're fighting the good fight. That you can win this war and take this city back."

"Don't they say that to everyone?"

For someone about to cut him down, the soldier's gaze remained sympathetic. Poor stupid rookie. "They do. But very few believe it by the time they come out of the other side. You'll see that when you've fought for years and seen no change."

"You say that like I have a future."

"Were I in your situation right now—"

"Weaponless and standing at the mercy of an experienced soldier with a sword?"

The soldier pulled in a deep breath before letting it go again. He spoke measured words, his tone as soft as his kind gaze. "Were *I* in your situation, I'd see I had the advantage. That I was closest to the only way out of this room."

The door leading to the hallway on Reuben's left.

"*I'd* think about where the soldiers and drones were last, and recognise they walked away from the front of this house. *I'd* go out the back. *I'd* thank my lucky stars, and *I'd* think twice about any further encounter I have with Fear's soldiers. I might focus on the similarities between them and myself rather than the differences. I might show them the same kindness I was being shown right now. Sure, they're from a different city, but they're still sent outside its walls to fight a war without end. They're still lied to by those in power to make them believe their sacrifice will force some kind of change. That it will make the world a safer place for future generations." The man shrugged. "But I'm not very smart. How can I be to get myself in his situation where I have a sword, but I'm at a disadvantage? So maybe what I'd do isn't very important or the best course of action."

Reuben stepped towards the open doorway on his left, his fingers splayed as if testing the air around him for the soldier's deceit. He'd spent too much time with Hicks. Was the man playing a cruel trick on him? Just one step at first. Like entering a cold pool, he dipped his toe in.

The soldier sighed and tapped his foot.

Reuben took another step left.

The soldier remained still.

The next step took Reuben out into the hallway. "Thank you," he said.

The soldier shrugged. "I don't understand why you're thanking me."

Reuben turned his back on the living room and ran through the old kitchen at the rear of the house. Many of the metal appliances were pockmarked with rust, but maintained their form. Every cupboard had been reduced to a doorless and rotting carcass.

The back garden was a dust bowl of neglect. What remained of the back fence stood as five-foot-tall concrete pillars.

The moon continued to shine bright enough to guide him. The soldier still hadn't given chase. He ran faster. He needed to get away from there. Had he been set up? Would this turn out to be a trap? Some kind of sick game? When would he hear the drones' hum? Reuben shrugged. What did he have to lose by running? Maybe they were toying with him. But what were his options? He could either run, or remain in the house and have a sword driven through his stomach. At least if he ran, he had a chance.

CHAPTER 22

Reuben ached from ankles to temples by the time he reached the road leading to Fury's gates. He itched all over. His skin had turned tacky from where he'd sweated and it had dried again several times. He stumbled and shivered, hugging himself for warmth. But he'd returned, and he was still alive. Regardless of what he'd been through and witnessed, he'd been lucky tonight. And if the narrative sold to him about Fear's soldiers and their violent tendencies were true, he'd been very lucky. He'd met one of the few good eggs out there. What would have happened had he run into someone like Danko with a vicious bitch like Hicks whispering in his ear?

The imposing steel gates remained closed. The first time he'd returned to the city without them opening automatically. He knocked with a shaking hand, the cold and hard steel stinging his knuckles.

The strong wind called across the city. The flapping of a bird's wings as it took flight. Dawn still a few hours away, the ruins now lay dormant.

He knocked again.

A letterbox-sized hatch shifted to one side with a *snap!* The open gap framed a pair of scowling eyes. "What do you want?"

"Isn't it obvious?"

"Don't get smart with me, *boy*. Why are you coming back at this time?"

"I got separated from my unit."

"A deserter?"

"Doesn't deserter suggest I'd be heading *away* from the city?"

"What did I say about getting smart? I can leave you outside until morning if you want, rookie?"

"Hicks?"

"Who else?"

"What are you doing on guard duty?"

"I'm the one who asks the questions."

The surrounding city remained clear. And it might stay that way, even if Fear's army came close. They might have hungered for war, but it would be suicide to attack someone outside Fury's gates. But the diseased didn't understand boundaries and the likelihood of a city's very capable defence. The second they saw him, they'd charge. If that happened, the gates would most certainly stay closed. "Will you please let me in?"

A voice came from behind Hicks. Male, it resonated with a bass note boom. "Who is it?"

"No one," Hicks said.

A different pair of eyes stared through the slot. Sarge's cold steel gaze.

Reuben stood to attention, his arms at his sides. He continued to shiver. He needed a shower, some food, and a good eight hours' sleep.

"Oh. It's you."

Two bolts released on the other side of the gate. *Crack! Crack!* The hinges on one side cackled as it opened.

The second the gap had stretched wide enough, Reuben slipped inside.

Before Reuben had stepped through, Hicks slammed the gate shut, catching the back of his heels. She glared at him while re-securing the locks. *Crack! Crack!*

Sarge stepped forwards and stopped just inches from Reuben. He folded his thick arms and looked him up and down. "So what happened?"

"I got caught by one of Fear's soldiers."

"Why are you still here, then?"

"They let me go."

Hicks gasped.

"To spy on us?"

"*No!*" Reuben edged back a step. "He said he didn't want to kill me. He didn't put any conditions on my life. He said he didn't believe in the war. That enough people had died. That he saw no point in killing a rookie." Reuben shot a glance at Hicks, who straightened her back, rolled her shoulders, and then cleared her throat.

Sarge harrumphed before he said, "And what happened in the car park?"

"Drones," Reuben said. "Hasn't Hicks already told you?"

"I want to hear it from you."

"We were taking a break when a swarm of drones came down into the car park. We were the only unit who got away. It was a massacre. Hicks led us down to the lower level so we could hide in the shadows."

Sarge spun his hand through the air, turning it over to encourage Reuben to continue. "Go on."

"Well …" Hicks edged a step closer to Reuben. He'd best pick his words carefully. Tomorrow, they'd be outside the walls with one another again. "We avoided them. We doubled back so we could return to the top car park."

"But …?"

He glanced at Hicks again. "There was a drone waiting on the ramp out of there."

"And what did you do, hero?" Hicks said.

Heat spread through Reuben's cheeks. He bowed his head and addressed Sarge's boots. "I took down the drone so we could get free."

"Did you ask if that was the right thing to do?"

"No, Sarge. I used my initiative. It was a tricky situation, and we didn't have much time."

Sarge's voice grew louder. "Did anyone *ask* you to use your initiative?"

Reuben shook his head.

"So why do it? Are you so arrogant that you think *your* initiative has any worth?"

"We needed a way out of there, and I saw a chance."

"Which separated you from your team and alerted all the other drones to your presence." He sighed before lifting his shoulders in a shrug. "I mean, at least all of your team got away."

"Grov—"

Sarge snapped his head to one side. His interest piqued.

He couldn't only ask about her. "Great," Reuben said.

Hicks snorted a laugh.

"I'm pleased the rest of the team made it back."

"Despite your best attempts to prevent that," Hicks said.

Sarge rubbed his temples as if fighting off a headache. "I dread to think what it would have been like had your stupidity killed some of them."

"But it worked."

Sarge stamped his foot and leaned close. His furious breath slammed into Reuben. "Not because of you! Did you know the dogs were coming? Did you know Danko had pressed his call button, and even if you guessed that, did you know they'd be there in time to save your arse?"

Reuben returned his attention to Sarge's boots.

Hicks turned her palms to the sky. "Well?" She sounded like she struggled to contain her mirth.

"No."

Sarge said, "So let's play out a different scenario."

"I'd rather not."

"Did I ask what you'd rather do?"

Reuben shook his head. "No."

"So what would have happened if the dogs hadn't arrived?"

"The drones would have attacked me."

"And maybe the rest of your team?" Hicks said.

"Oh, I doubt that." Reuben glared at Hicks. "They were well hidden at that point. I don't think the drones would have found them. They got away quickly."

Hicks raised a balled fist. Her small teeth bared in a now all too familiar expression. "You expected us to put our lives at risk for *you?*"

"When the dogs engaged the drones in combat, you could have come out of hiding and shown me where you were."

"You needed to learn."

"So you *were* watching me?"

"Actually"—Hicks shook her head—"we weren't. We assumed you were dead. The second we left the car park, we ran and didn't look back."

Ushering Hicks aside with a sweep of his right arm, Sarge pointed his thick index finger at Reuben. It hovered inches from his face. "What you need to learn from this is the only thing that kept you alive was dumb luck. Nothing else. Don't go thinking you did anything brave or smart out there because you didn't. Your actions didn't save anyone. The dogs were on their way, and had you stopped to consult with your leader, you would have discovered that."

And they would have been caught on the wrong side of an underground battle between the two. Reuben kept the thought to himself.

"Next time, check with someone in charge before you act, okay? Chances are their plans are better than yours." He sighed and rested a hand on Reuben's shoulder. His tone softened. "Experience counts for everything in the ruined city. You understand?"

Reuben leaned into the man's touch. "I do. Thank you. And you know what else was lucky?"

Sarge raised one eyebrow.

"Me meeting a compassionate soldier in Fear's army. He could have cut my throat, or worse."

"And he should have." Sarge's hand fell away. He turned his back on Reuben and called back over his shoulder, "This is war. If you're not ruthless, you're dead." He turned to face him again and stabbed the same accusatory finger in his direction. "If you tell anyone about what happened with Fear's army, I will make you wish they'd tortured you."

"But—"

"Reuben," Hicks said as Sarge walked away, "you'd do well to learn when it's best to shut the fuck up."

CHAPTER 23

The early morning dew had already turned Reuben's clothes damp. He then made the mistake of sitting down beneath the bridge. While the large canopy might have offered protection against rain, the dew soaked the ground here the same as it would anywhere else. The seat of his trousers were now sodden.

At the bottom of the steep bank, the river rushed along, its dark surface tipped with streaks of white. The strong wind drilled into Reuben, who hugged his knees to his chest. The same dew that coated everything else glistened on Malcolm's crimson blanket. Yet the man beneath it slept like the dead.

Reuben stretched a tentative hand towards his friend. But before he made contact, Malcolm exploded to life. He slammed into Reuben and knocked him on his back. He raised a balled fist. His eyes and mouth stretched wide. The bridge's acoustics amplified his yell.

"Malcolm, it's me."

"Reuben?" Malcolm frowned but kept his fist raised. His chest rose and fell in heavy waves. The man might have been

Reuben's senior by a good few years, but there'd only ever be one winner if it kicked off. What he lacked in power, he more than made up for with experience. He blinked repeatedly as if his eyes weren't working. Where his yell had been crystal clear, his voice now crackled with fatigue. "What time is it?"

The air had turned grainy in the weak light. The day had transitioned from pitch black to dark blue. The promise of the rising sun stretched through Fury. "About four in the morning."

"What are you doing here?"

"I'm sorry, but you said if I ever needed to talk … no matter the time of day."

Malcolm fell into a sitting position with a squelch. Much like Reuben had, he pulled his knees into his chest, the best way to brace against the steep slope and keep warm. He ran his hand through his unruly white hair. He coughed several times, his lungs damp. "That I did."

"You just didn't expect me at this time of day?"

"Doesn't mean I'm not ready to listen." Malcolm flicked his chin up. "So what's going on?"

"I've had a rough night."

"You've been outside the city?"

"Yeah."

"Who died?"

"Lots of people, actually. Fear's drones found us in an underground car park. My unit were the only ones who got away."

"That's rough."

"And then I got separated from them. They left me."

"What?"

"I thought I was helping, but they said my actions were stupid. That I put everyone in danger and I was a liability.

And maybe I was. I acted quickly. I took down a drone that stood in our way."

"And you succeeded?"

"Yeah."

"I don't get it. What was the problem, then?"

"I didn't consult anyone. I just acted. But I felt like something needed to happen quickly."

"Doesn't sound to me like you're the one who's at fault."

There seemed little point in going over it again. Regardless of the reality, Hicks and Sarge told him he'd been in the wrong, and as far as his military career went, they were the only opinions that mattered. "Then Fear's army caught me."

"Jeez. Sounds like a lot happened. But if Fear's army caught you, why are you still here?"

"They let me go."

"*What?*"

"Well, one of them did. A soldier in his late twenties to early thirties. He had a few years' service under his belt. A calmer head than some younger soldiers. He said he'd grown tired of all the killing. And not that I'd admit this in front of the others, but I can see why."

"And that's why you're still here? That's something, right?"

Reuben breathed in through his nose. The underside of the bridge reeked of damp mud and salt. "Yeah. He was a nice guy. He saw I was a rookie and let me go. But when I came back and told Sarge, he told me to forget it had ever happened and there'd be consequences if I told anyone."

"Of course he did."

Reuben raised an eyebrow.

"What good is it for Fury's army to see the enemy as just like us? As human too? The next step is for them to realise they're fighting in a pointless war. And what happens then? We talk to one another? We refuse to fight. We agree on a truce? Do that and someone like Sarge ceases to exist. If there's no war, he has no purpose. None of the military leaders do. Or the current batch of politicians."

"You think this war would be that easy to stop?"

"I think it's pointless. I think those in power are fearful of other people coming to that conclusion. They have the run of the city because they keep the people safe. Take away the threat, and the citizens will want more from their leaders. If they feel secure, they'll want a quality of life they've been deprived of until this point. It wouldn't surprise me to hear they're working in tandem with the high-ups in Fear. They're probably talking right now after the trick that soldier pulled. What can they do to escalate the tensions again? How many more soldiers will they sacrifice to ensure their citizens remain petrified?"

"That's a bold claim."

"Maybe. But tell me it doesn't make sense. Keep the citizens scared and grateful, and they'll never question your actions or motives."

Reuben ran a hand over his head and fixed on the rushing river, his focus blurring. He scratched the back of his neck, his skin tacky with dried sweat. "Even if that's not true—"

"You don't think it's true?"

"I don't know." Reuben shrugged. "It makes sense, but I just don't know. *But,* even if that isn't true, I still don't know if I have it in me. This war, I mean. I don't know if I can believe in it. It makes it hard to fight when I'm outside the walls. I'm not like Hicks or Danko. I can't see myself ever torturing someone to death. There's not enough hatred in my heart, and I never want to be in a place where there is. Especially after what happened tonight."

"That might be an unpopular opinion, but that doesn't make it wrong. The sane man is the unreasonable one when drowning in a narrative of madness." Malcolm clapped a hand against Reuben's back. "Believe me, there are some nutters in our military. Proper fucking fanatics. And, unfortunately, they're the ones who rise to the top. They have the zeal to keep pushing the agenda. They have the lack of empathy to not give a damn about morals. The powers that be need people like that to help maintain the status quo. But if you're in it for the right reasons, maybe you need to accept the peaks and troughs that come with the job?"

"I thought you just said it was all bullshit?"

"That's just my opinion. You have your own mind. Maybe, as someone on the inside, you can be the change you'd like to see. Just remember, if you don't like it, do your ninety days and leave."

"But it's all I've ever wanted."

"That's not a reason to stay. Now you're better informed, it's okay to change your mind. Nothing turns out as we expect. Also, you don't have to decide today. You still have several months ahead of you. If you leave, there's no shame in that. It's better to walk away than persevere with something you hate. No matter how you look at it, if it's not right for you in your heart, nothing else matters."

"How do I know what's right in my heart?"

"Listen to it. Notice how you're feeling. When it comes time to make a choice, you'll know what to do. True misery comes from living a life counter to your heart's desires. And I'm speaking from experience."

"Thanks, Malcolm." Reuben's bottom had turned numb on the cold and damp slope. "I'm sorry I woke you."

"It's not like I have much on tomorrow."

"Can I ask you something?"

"You just did."

"Where do all of your opinions come from? You never tell me much about you."

"Where do you think I got my red blanket?"

"I don't understand."

"I'm ex-military, Reuben."

Reuben's mind spun. He might have been seated, but he still pressed a stabilising hand against the muddy ground to keep himself upright. He shook his head. *"What?* Why didn't you tell me?"

"Would it have made a difference?"

Reuben paused. "No, I don't suppose it would. I needed to do this."

"We all have to tread our own path. What's wrong for me might be right for you. What purpose would it have served if I'd been constantly negative about the military? Especially when you had your heart set on it. But now I've told you …" Malcolm got to his feet. "I want to show you something."

They emerged from beneath the bridge and walked along the riverbank. The wind cut across the city and slammed into their right sides. Reuben stumbled. A much harder gust would have sent him into the frigid water below.

The sky had turned a lighter shade of blue, the sun's yellow tinge on the horizon. They reached the next bridge along the river. Malcolm pushed a finger to his lips before he hunched down and pointed under. Three more crimson blankets like the one he slept beneath. They covered three more veterans.

They walked into town in silence. Anything they said would carry and disturb the slumbering city. Dark and dead-end alleyways, they had more red blankets stretched along them. Old vets slept huddled behind large bins. There were some in the park. Some of them slept beneath benches; some were out in the open. It took for Reuben to squint to see them all, many of the vets choosing shadowy spots to remain inconspicuous.

On their way back to the bridge, when they'd left the city

far enough behind, Reuben spoke in a whisper. "Why am I only finding out about this now?"

"You know the rules; don't go out at night. Unless you're in the military, and even then it should only be when you're coming back from a shift."

"But they're *everywhere*," Reuben said. "Other people must have seen them."

"The easiest life in this city is the one that kicks up the least amount of fuss. Stick your head above the parapet and people will take potshots at it." Malcolm lifted his wide and bony shoulders in a shrug. "And we play our part well. We're a stain on this society. We have to make sure we're discreet if we want to retain the privilege of living here."

"But you're *heroes*."

Malcolm frowned at Reuben.

"Sorry." Reuben lowered his voice. "But you're heroes."

"No, we're not. People like Sarge are heroes. People who devote their life to the cause. We're a drain on the system. The uniform is the symbol of heroism, not the people wearing it. The uniform can never get old and washed up. The uniform will never turn its back on the military. When we can't or don't want to fight anymore, we take it off. We become civvies. Tired, jaded, broken, and washed-up civvies. We become worthless. Most of us who have done any kind of time in the army need a while to get our heads together when we return to normal life. Many of us can't work because of physical issues. Many because of mental issues. You try working in the local butchers, hacking chunks off flesh from carcasses, when you've seen what we have."

"And what about you?" Reuben said. "You seem well."

Malcolm tapped the side of his head with his index finger. He shrugged. "I left a lot of myself outside those walls, and I've been trying to get it back. I'm not there yet."

"So while you're getting yourself together, that's when you fall through the cracks?"

"Yeah, with no help and no support, we plunge into a cycle of homelessness. Your girlfriend's dad is lucky to have someone looking after him."

"She's not my girlfriend."

"It's just a matter of time."

"There must be other options. After you've given so much, surely the city will help you?"

"For those who have no one to help them, there's always the pill."

"The pill?"

"It's quick and easy. Solves all your problems."

"Shit!"

"Yeah."

"Do many take it?"

"Yeah." They closed in on Malcolm's bridge. "I'm sorry to tell you all this, Reuben. I thought it was the right time."

"How do the people of Fury not know about this?"

"If you're not in the military, which the bulk of people aren't, then you stay in at night and you never see the vets."

"What about all the people who do serve in the military?"

"They know to keep their mouths shut. They know what's good for them. That's the other thing I've been meaning to tell you. You can't speak out about this. Much like you can't talk about what happens outside the walls. What *really* happens, I mean. The torture. The underhanded nature of warfare. The people of Fury need to think this is a valiant war. That the people fighting it are true heroes rather than sadists and psychopaths."

"And if I do speak out about it?"

"It won't end well for you. But you still have a choice, and I wanted to make sure it's an informed choice. The military might be for you, and no judgement if it is, but if not, you can have a better life than I've had. If, after ninety days, it isn't right, then don't sign up. Work in the fields. The factories. The butchers."

The girl's punctured eye stared at Reuben from his memories. Her severed ear. "Thanks, Malcolm. And I'm sorry for what's happened to you."

"You've nothing to be sorry for. It's not your fault. In fact, you've done more for me than anyone in this city. If they had someone like you in charge, I'm sure it would be a very different story."

"And maybe that's a reason to stay? Force change from the inside?"

"It's that or lead a revolution. But it's hard to revolt when very few people see the need. They'll keep sending their kids to soldiers to thank them for their service, and they'll remain grateful every day. As long as the war doesn't make it into the city, then what do they have to complain about?"

Reuben's head spun. "Everything I ever knew was a lie."

"Not everything." Malcolm hugged him. "But a lot of it is."

Reuben broke away. "I need to get some sleep. We're back outside the walls again soon. I'll get your sandwich to you later, okay?"

"Do me a favour, leave it for today, yeah? Rest and recover."

"But—"

"Honestly, I don't need it today."

"Thanks again, Malcolm."

"See you soon, son."

The tall man hunched as he ducked under his bridge and vanished into the shadows. Maybe Malcolm needed a son just as much as Reuben needed a father.

CHAPTER 24

The start of a new day, the sun delivering an eye-stinging reminder to Reuben of how little time he had left before they were due back outside the city's walls. How little sleep he'd get when he arrived home. He'd nearly gotten them killed last night. How much of a liability would he be when he went out again with so little rest?

And of course Sarge didn't think he'd earned a day off, despite coming back much later than the others. Despite being left high and dry by his unit. Or, more likely, by Hicks, who would have persuaded Danko to lead them away from the car park the second they emerged. He could have visited Malcolm another time, but he'd needed to see him. Needed someone to help him rearrange his thoughts. Although, after Malcom's guided tour of the city and revelation about what happened to those who'd served in the military ...

How had the city kept the homeless vets a secret from the rest of the population? They'd convinced the people of Fury that staying in at night had always been a choice. A choice with consequences if they didn't comply, but a choice all the same. Why go out after dark anyway? Everything shut down for the evening. Unless you were a soldier, what need did you have to move around at night? What were you doing wrong?

What would Reuben do at the end of his ninety days? The military had been his sole focus for years. Without that, what did he have? But could he keep fighting a savage war without end, purpose, or morals? A war neither side could, or were meant to win. Were the batons and knives a choice made by the leaders of the two cities? Arm the soldiers with guns and flamethrowers and things would get resolved fast. After all, they had dogs and drones. Did they come from another society, or did both Fear and Fury make them themselves? A few of each to help maintain balance. To give the dumb soldiers a shot of confidence as they left the safety of their city's walls. With what he now knew and what he suspected, how could he even consider signing on for life when his three months were up?

Reuben's home occupied the ground floor of what had once been a small two-bedroom house. It had been converted into two bedsits. The entrance to his place sat around the side of the small building where the old back door used to be. He halted when he rounded the corner. "Groves? What are you doing here?"

"Reuben!" She'd been sat on his doorstep. She jumped to her feet and walked towards him. Her skin pale, she had bags that looked like bruises beneath her eyes.

"Have you slept?"

Groves threw her arms wide and wrapped him in a tight hug. She pulled back and looked from one of his eyes to the other, her own glazed and swelling with tears. "You're alive! I knew you were. I had a feeling you were all right." She shook her head and blinked, which ran two damp tracks down her cheeks. "I'm so sorry."

"What are you talking about?"

"I'm sorry we left you behind."

"What were you going to do? Wait for the drones to attack you because I'd led them all from the car park? I nearly got you all killed. I was stupid. If the dogs hadn't turned up, I would have died and deserved it. How long have you been waiting here?"

"When we got back from our run-in with the drones, I went home to check on Dad and Annabelle before heading over. So what happened to you?"

"It's a long story, and you need to sleep. We're going out again in a few hours. As much as I'd love to hang out with you, neither of us will be grateful for this time when we're on patrol later. I've nearly killed you once with those drones. I won't do it again by contributing to your sleep deprivation."

Groves held both of Reuben's hands. Her grip warmed his own.

Wobbling where he stood, Reuben's head pounded and his throat dried. But he had to say it. What better chance would he get? "Uhh …" Every trip outside the gates could be the one that ended him. Or her. "I'd … I mean … I …" He leaned towards her, fighting against his own self-doubt. What if she rejected him?

But Groves met him halfway, pressing her lips to his.

Reuben's fatigue vanished, driven away by the sweet contact of her soft kiss.

When they pulled apart, Reuben said, "I've wanted that to happen since I met you."

Groves smiled. "Me too."

"Will you tell me your name now?"

Groves shook her head. "You need that to ask me out on a date. This *isn't* a date!" The slightest smile lifted the rest of her tired face. She leaned in and kissed him again. "I'm so glad you're okay. See you later, yeah?"

"Yeah." Reuben nodded.

Groves walked away.

Reuben smiled when she turned around, and then released a hard sigh as she vanished from sight. He opened his front door and fell into his small bedsit. He'd get an hour's sleep. Not great, but better than nothing. He shed his clothes in a line that led from his door to his bed and fell onto the soft mattress face first. His mind ran laps of his skull. He didn't have to decide for a few months, but could he really leave the military now? Had Groves just given him the best reason to stay?

CHAPTER 25

Every step loaded with reluctance and exhaustion, Reuben fell into his clumsy jog on his way to the front gates. Before he'd started national service, he'd been able to run for days, but his lack of sleep had left his body unresponsive and his chest tight. Nausea balled a fist around his stomach, and every time one of his feet slammed down, his throbbing brain rattled in his skull. He would have been better off not sleeping at all. The hour in bed only showed him what he'd missed out on now he had to report for duty.

The units were lined up before the already open gates. The first line of five on the left were exiting the city. Fortunately, his team remained.

Groves stood at the back of the line. She half-turned to him and spoke from the side of her mouth. "I dallied a little to give you time to get here."

"Thank you." Reuben leaned forwards, his hands on his knees to help him breathe.

But he had no time for rest, his team setting off a second later. As he passed Sarge, Reuben leaned away, repelled by the heat radiating from the man's scolding disdain.

A few metres clear of the gates, Reuben called ahead, "Groves, thank you for waiting for me last night. It's made everything else worthwhile."

Hicks slowed down, killing any chance of a conversation and forcing Reuben and Groves to catch her. Her green eyes were dead. "Don't think I didn't notice you were late."

The reply left Reuben's mouth before he caught it. "I don't give a shit what you noticed. You're not in charge of this unit."

Another unit passed them while Hicks ran her tongue around the inside of her mouth. She pointed her finger at Reuben. "You need to watch yourself, rookie."

"Are you telling me I'm wrong? Shall we check?" He cupped his mouth with his hands. "Hey, Danko…"

Their bald leader had halted a few feet ahead with Hernandez. His rounded shoulders were raised, thickening the back of his neck as if his hard scowl started in the middle of his shoulder blades, crawled over the back of his head, and pushed his brow down to his chin.

Reuben pointed at Hicks with the thumb of his right hand. "You need to watch this one. She's talking like she's in charge of this unit. I'd keep an eye on that knife she carries in case it ends up in your back."

Hicks' thin lips receded. "You've crossed the line, rookie. Don't think I'll forget about this anytime soon."

"Fuck off, Hicks." Groves gasped. But fuck Hicks. Whether he left at the end of his ninety days or not, he wouldn't take her shit any longer.

Growing redder by the second, Hicks once again jabbed a finger at him. But the words never left her open mouth.

The explosion shook the ground, and Danko took off in its direction.

On her way back to the front of the unit, Hicks called

back over her shoulder, "Don't think I'll forget your insolence, rookie."

~

About twenty of Fury's soldiers had already reached the explosion site. They'd been planted in a different road to the one Reuben had previously seen. They were much closer to the edge of the city. Eight dogs paced between them. Enough to deter the drones, or at least deal with the threat should it arrive. Many of the soldiers had their batons raised, and they scanned their surroundings. But whatever had triggered the landmine had gone.

"That's strange."

Reuben leaned close to Groves. "What is?"

"I'd expect to find the splattered remains of a diseased at the very least. Sometimes, if we're lucky, we find one of Fear's soldiers painted across a wall."

"Lucky?"

"You think they'll have a better end if they're still alive?"

"No, I suppose not."

"It's quick. It's all you can hope for if you die in this city. But—" Groves pointed at the charred ground and then looked up and down the street "—there's no evidence of what triggered the mine."

The loud *clang* of metal being struck a street or two away. The dogs took off, their *clack-clack* leading the charge.

Groves shook her head. "This doesn't feel right."

But Danko had already joined the other leaders in following the dogs.

"You should say something," Reuben said.

"To those two?"

"Why not? It might save their lives."

"I'm not sure they've ever been receptive to *anything* before. What makes you think they will be now?"

And he couldn't blame her for not wanting to speak up. Life under the rule of Hicks by proxy had little patience for ideas and opinions.

Two streets away, the dogs slowed their pace. Shops on either side of the main road, those along their right side had statues on the roofs. They were the ones they'd previously seen from a different vantage point. Now they loomed over them. Sinister and predatory, they would have made sure the citizens of the old city knew what they had to sell and that they damn well bought it. A large *M* on one, a smiling face on another, a chicken, a donut.

Like every soldier there, Reuben scanned the roofs for signs of a retreating enemy. Had they gone through the sewers while everyone watched the sky? Adrenaline had driven away his fatigue, but his breathing remained laboured. Before he could catch it, the dogs set off again on something's trail. The leaders followed them, and he followed the leaders. They ran down an alley toward a tall metal tower. The structure had been one of the few to not fall victim to the virus of gnawing corrosion that had infected every other building he'd come across.

The front runners roared. Reuben and the others quickened their pace. They broke from an alley and found the reason for the charge. They'd found one of Fear's soldiers and gave chase. A solitary figure dressed in blue. As solitary as Reuben had been the previous evening. If they caught the man, they wouldn't spare him. With the number of Fury's soldiers present, they'd probably make him more of an example. The punishment could last for hours. And what could Reuben do about it? Like any of them would listen to the pleas of a rookie.

Fury's army carried a wall of sound with their charge. The *clack, clack* of the dogs underpinned the war cry.

Again, the front runners rounded the bend ahead of Reuben. Again, their sound revealed what lay in wait. Or, rather, their lack of sound. A moment of utter silence. Not even a second, but it lasted forever and spoke volumes.

Reuben halted the second he saw it. They were outnumbered at least five to one.

The hum of Fear's drones. There were twice as many as Fury had dogs.

The blue-uniformed army released a war cry that humiliated the one Fury had led with.

A stampede flooded forwards. A force too great to overcome.

"Shit!" Groves said, tugging on Reuben's arm, dragging him away and breaking him from his stunned paralysis. "We need to get out of here now."

CHAPTER 26

Would Reuben have stayed and fought had Groves not pulled him away? Hard to say for sure, but he'd not yet spent long enough in Fury's army to lose all his good sense. There were too many of them. Even if he and his comrades fought like angry gods, they had no chance of winning this battle. Thankfully, a few seconds after he and Groves retreated, the rest of Fury's soldiers came to the same realisation.

The *whomp* of the dogs' flaming attack bought them a few more seconds, a wall of searing heat that held Fear's soldiers back. The stuttered burst of the drones' Gatling guns responded, the ting of bullets hitting metal bodies. The battle between the machines threw up an impassible screen of conflict, but it would rescind, and when it did, there would only be one winner. Fury's only hope lay in how much of a distance they could put between them and their enemy.

Where Danko's unit had been near the back of Fury's army, they now led the retreat. All of them save Hicks. Almost every other soldier ran for their lives, but she stopped with several others, forming a line between Fury's retreat and the enemy. Fear were armed with either batons, knives, or poles. If the drones overcame the dogs, they'd get mowed down where they stood.

Reuben glanced back in time to see a hole appear in the dog's shielding wall of fire. Some of the mechanised canines were already down. Hicks and the others shifted across so they stood before it. She led the cry and threw her knife into the gap. "You shall not pass!"

Before she could yell again, one of Fear's soldiers burst through the smoke. He silenced her with a baton blow to the head. *Tonk!* Her knees buckled. As the gap in the flames grew, at least a hundred blue uniforms flooded the main street, burying Hicks and her brave band of fools.

"Look!"

Groves pointed at the rooftops. Two teenagers ran with them. They were either tracking their escape or fleeing Fear's army. Dressed as civvies, the boy and girl jumped from one building to the next.

Hernandez and Danko caught up to Reuben and Groves. Fear's army had ripped through Hicks and her band of brave idiots. The front runners were faster than anyone in Danko's unit and ate away at their lead.

"We're not going to make it," Hernandez said.

His face puce, Danko looked back.

"I know you don't want to hear it," Reuben said, "but if we stay with the rest of our army, we'll die."

"Fuck it!" Danko yelled. He slowed down, allowing two units to pass them. "Follow me." He peeled away and ducked down the next alley on their right.

A shop on one side, a tall warehouse on their right. One window in the warehouse's wall, the ledge about five feet from the ground. Danko dived through it into the large building.

Hernandez and then Groves followed him through.

Reuben reached the window last. Too dark to see what waited for them on the other side. But what else could he do? He stretched his hands out in front of him and dived into the unknown.

Danko and Groves caught Reuben on the other side. Hernandez stood back, her hand to her forehead. Blood streamed down her face. The ground crunched with broken glass; it shone like glitter on her wound.

"Come on." Danko ran to the other side of the warehouse. The window lower and taller, he jumped up onto the ledge and leaped out into the next alley.

CHAPTER 27

The screams from the main road rang through the city. Fury's soldiers were falling to Fear's attack. Danko's unit might have evaded them for now, but they were by no means safe. They'd bought time, but they weren't back inside their city's walls.

Danko had led them left from the old warehouse. They were back out in a wider street. Flanked on either side by shops, Reuben filled in the blanks. In his mind, he replaced the windows. He re-erected the signs. He added the people. No conflict, just a busy, functioning high street. But the wind soon shoved his imagination aside. It played the large empty structures with a deep bass hum. It resonated with abandonment. The road, just like every other asphalt surface in the crumbling city, had cracks along it with streaks of green grass packing the breaks. A promise of this city's future soundtracked by its wailing requiem.

Danko led them through another alley. Farther away from Fear's army and Fury's massacre. With the three tall towers at their back, they were also going farther away from home.

Reuben remained at the rear, and just before he reached their next alley, a toot of a loud horn snapped his attention to his left. A soldier in a blue uniform. "Fuck it!" The alley amplified Reuben's call. "They're onto us, Danko."

Danko jumped at the metal fire escape on his left and climbed. No time to argue. The team followed, Reuben still at the back and the last one to the roof.

The gaps between each building were small enough to clear with their large steps. All the roofs were flat. Fear responded to the horn, their numbers swelling in the street down to their left. The metal top of another fire escape was three buildings away on their right.

Groves and Reuben overtook Hernandez. Danko had already started his descent. Groves followed him, and Reuben paused. The blood from Hernandez's wound mixed with her sweat, covering her face with a mask of pink.

Hernandez clawed at her eyes. "I can't see!"

Although he had one foot on the fire escape, Reuben returned to the roof's white gravel. But a tug from behind stopped him going any farther. Groves pulled him back. Her eyes wide, she pointed at the drone rising on the opposite side of the building. The top half of the machine visible, the high-pitched whine of its screaming guns overrode its humming propellors.

The second it lifted above the roof, the ends of its guns turned into orange circles of heat.

"No!" Reuben's stomach lurched as Hernandez shook and twisted.

He pulled against Groves, who held on with both hands and tugged him back. "You can't help her," she said. "You can only save yourself now."

Reuben twisted again, this time breaking free.

Hernandez dropped to her knees. She fell forward into the gravel.

The air left Reuben's lungs. His stomach sank. His body slumped. His eyes glazed. His throat burned. "Hernandez." The woman who'd looked out for him from day one. If she'd been able to see, she'd have made it. If he'd noticed sooner, he'd have been able to help. If—

Groves had climbed onto the roof with Reuben. She yanked him back towards the fire escape.

The drone turned their way. Its guns whirred.

This time, Reuben followed, ducking in time to avoid the white-hot streaks of bullets flying over the top of his head.

CHAPTER 28

Sheer will carried Reuben down the fire escape's flight of metal stairs, the railing at the bottom preventing his fall. He should have noticed Hernandez had been blinded. He should have done more.

"Come on, Reuben!" Groves waited at the bottom of the next flight. "You need to keep moving."

By the time Reuben had stumbled down the stairs to the next level, Groves and Danko had already vaulted over the side. A ten-foot drop to the road below. His vision blurred and his tight throat forced his breaths out in wheezing gasps. He grabbed the metal railing and threw himself over. The shock of his clumsy landing sent a twinge up his back, his legs failed him, and he slammed down onto his knees.

Danko grabbed Reuben beneath his armpits and pulled him to his feet. He glanced at the building they'd just run across as if he could see through it to the army on the other side. He said, "We need to get back to Fury as soon as possible." His large bald head shone with sweat, and his words dripped with uncertainty. Lost without Hicks telling him what to do. But he had to decide. His focus returned, and he snapped a sharp nod. "You need to follow me. Okay?"

The collective hum of drones travelled across the top of the building. The roar of Fear's army shot down the several alleys they'd entered to get to them. Danko led them away.

A metal ramp about one hundred feet from them, Danko reached it first. It ran a snaking path to an elevated walkway crossing an old train line. Covered in wire mesh, the bridge led to a train yard. Several rusting metal carcasses were all that remained of a long-abandoned industry. A vast ugly building loomed on their left. It had been built across the train track.

The drones were already gaining on them, and most of the soldiers had made it through the alleys. Instead of following the ramp, Danko took the most direct route. He vaulted several handrails in his path, each one higher than the one preceding it. Groves followed him. Reuben took up the rear, slipping on the first railing, slamming his shin against the metal barrier, and falling flat on his back onto the walkway. But he stumbled to his feet again, got up, and pushed on.

The *whir* of Gatling guns. That all too familiar sound. The *ting* of bullets hitting the metal on the bridge all around them. It wound his torso tight, and he flinched as he ran, expecting the searing assault to chew into his back.

Danko and Groves waited in the tunnel for Reuben. His shins on fire, his back aching, his throat still taut with grief. He fell forward as the *ting* of more bullets lit up the walkway.

"They'll get us if we come out on the other side," Danko said. He turned left down a path leading them into the ugly building.

The drones rose. Eight to ten of them, they moved as a swarm. A flood of blue uniforms filled the road, and the front runners had already reached the ramps.

Still at the back, Reuben followed the others into the ugly building's stairwell. A faded number six on the wall beside them. Danko had already gone from sight, Groves running halfway down the first flight of stairs before leaping the rest of the way, landing with a *crack,* turning one hundred and eighty degrees, and running to the next level below.

Following Groves, every landing slammed through Reuben's exhausted and throbbing body.

On the third floor, Danko waited for them to catch up before he kicked a door wide and plunged into a long corridor that ran from one side of the building to the other. Their destination, a door similar to the one they'd just burst through at the other end. Rooms sat on either side of the long symmetrical hallway. The white tiles on the floor had cracked and turned grey with age.

The rooms on either side looked like classrooms. Desks scattered throughout, each space had a focal point at the front. A spot for the teacher.

Danko pulled the door open at the other end and nipped through. Another stairwell. A carbon copy of the last. They climbed again, Danko's voice echoing in the cavernous space, "Going to ground is too predictable. I hope you have some more stairs in you?"

Reuben didn't have much of anything left, so what did it matter which way they went? He'd find what he needed when he needed it. Groves, as always, moved as if she flew, chewing up the stairs ahead of her in pursuit of Danko.

There were more stairs past the sixth floor. The seventh didn't have a number like the others. It led to a dead end, their climb culminating in a glassless window overlooking the city. Danko waited for Reuben to catch up, standing in the full force of the wind. "You both ready for this?"

Groves nodded. Reuben gulped back the thick saliva in his dry throat and copied her.

Danko climbed out of the window, reached up, and vanished from sight.

A flick of her head, Groves encouraged Reuben to go next.

The wind stung Reuben's already sore eyes and jabbed needles into his ears. He'd poked his head out between a crisscross of rusty metal bars that clung to the side of the building in the shape of a spider's web. Each bar an inch thick, Danko had shown they'd support his weight.

Reuben grabbed a bar and shook it to be sure. He watched where he put his feet, his head spinning because of how high they were. He stepped out of the window. The webbing held. He climbed after Danko, his stomach turning over on itself, the strength draining from his legs.

"We've seen this building plenty of times, but have never been in it before," Danko said, calling down to Reuben. "Dad told me it used to be a school. When they were building it, they ran a competition for the students to help with the design. The spiderweb won. And thank the heavens it did."

"Good for us at least," Reuben shouted back. He paused in his climb. Groves hadn't left the building yet. "Groves?"

She poked her head out.

"What are you doing?"

Her face pale, her eyes wide and bloodshot, she fought for breath. "I didn't know we'd have to climb."

"What are you talking about?"

"You need to leave me."

Reuben's grip weakened, and his stomach flipped. He hooked his arm through the bars to hold him in place. "What? No way!"

"I've been *shot*, Reuben." She pulled her head back into the building for several seconds. When she appeared again, tears filled her eyes and her mouth bent out of shape. "And Fear's soldiers are coming. The only way out of this is to climb."

"What? Why didn't you tell me you'd been shot? We could have gone another way."

"I didn't realise we'd have to climb."

"But …" Reuben shook his head. "No! You can do it. You have to at least *try*."

"I *won't* make it."

"But—"

Groves climbed from the building. She held on with her left hand and winced while she removed her top with her unresponsive right. There were two deep crimson holes in her arm. One in her bicep and one next to her wrist. They both belched thick blood. Her arm hung limp. "I *won't* make it. I can't climb like this. And you can't carry me."

"I can."

Groves smiled through her tears. "At least my dad will get his payout now. And he won't have to send his last daughter outside the city."

"No." Reuben shook his head. His throat burned. "No."

"It's Lisa, by the way."

"Lisa." He climbed down as he repeated her name back to her. But she let go. A sixty-foot drop to the ground. She fell backwards, turning over as she tumbled away from the building. She hit the concrete below with a *thud!* The impact ran through Reuben. His arm slipped from the rusting metal bar.

Danko reached down and caught Reuben's shoulder. He trembled with the effort and spoke through clenched teeth. "Come on, we need to get out of here."

If Reuben fell now, Danko would have a better chance. But he clung on again. A deep need to survive despite everything. He resumed his climb. The bars rough with rust. He pulled himself up, yelling with the effort of every action.

Danko pulled him the rest of the way. He dragged him onto the roof.

Lying on his front, shaking with his sobs, Reuben fell limp. How the hell could he carry on now?

CHAPTER 29

Reuben lay on his front, his body bouncing with his heavy sobs. Danko's steps tore away from him across the ridge of the steel roof. He halted after several feet. The man's form blurred through his tears, but Reuben made out his silhouette waving him on. "We've built up a lead. We need to make the most of it. Come on."

Every second on the roof gave the drones a better chance of finding them. Reuben shook with the effort of standing up. Stars swam in his vision, and he fell from one step into the next in pursuit of his leader.

Danko waited for Reuben at the other end. They overlooked the walkway with the wire mesh cover, about ten feet below them and six feet away from the edge of the building. His hands on his hips, his mouth stretched wide to help him breathe, Reuben said, "How the hell do we get down there?"

"We jump," Danko said. "Unless you have a better plan?"

The wind rocked Reuben where he stood. He should let it carry him off now.

The train station down to their left. Fear's soldiers must

have all been inside the building. They'd be on the roof soon enough.

"We jump now, or we lose our advantage," Danko said. "If we can get to that train station, we can get into the underground. I can get us back to Fury from there, and I'm confident we can lose them. You ready?"

"Do we have any other choice?" Reuben dragged in a damp sniff and wiped his nose with the back of his sleeve.

"If we do, I don't know what it is." Danko took both of Reuben's hands and stooped to force eye contact. "I know what Groves meant to you." The crazy had left him. A humanity sat in his compassionate gaze that Reuben wouldn't have believed existed until that moment. "And you need to let out your feelings, but not now." He shook his head. "Not here. Live first and then feel every ounce of this agony when it's safe."

The world blurred again, and Reuben's face buckled.

"You need to do this for her. It's what she would have wanted."

Reuben nodded. He needed to do it for her.

CHAPTER 30

Crash! Danko landed flatfooted on the wire mesh with his hands away from his sides for stability. The entire bridge shook from his landing and he swayed. The back of Reuben's knees weakened as he waited for his leader to fall. But he turned to Reuben and beckoned him down.

The longer he thought about it, the less likely he'd be to follow. He had to do this for Groves. And if he died trying, then so what? For Groves! The strength left his shaking legs, but Reuben jumped after him, yelling with the effort of boosting himself away from the roof. His stomach leaped into his throat as he fell. Rigid when he landed, the shock snapped through him. But he remained standing.

Danko gripped him by the top of his arms. A firm hold. He had him. He'd made it. "You good?"

The tracks fifty feet below were one of the few things in this city still in working order. They showed little sign of corrosion. They drew a dead straight line beneath the walkway and ran away from them in both directions. Reuben's world spun to look down for too long. He returned his attention to Danko. Should he fall now? End the pain? He gulped. "Yeah, I'm good."

The wire mesh of the tunnel's roof let out a rattling *whoosh!* Danko led the way along it at a sprint.

Reuben followed. If he looked down, especially at this pace, he'd fall.

They got to within ten feet of the end of the tunnel when the all too familiar hum of the drones' propellors joined them. The sound buzzed around them, thickening the air. It drilled into Reuben's skull. Get caught in the open and they had no defence. They'd get torn to shreds in seconds.

"Fuck!" Danko shouted while peering over his shoulder. He quickened his pace, jumped from the roof of the tunnel, cleared the first half of the snaking ramp leading to the ground, and landed on the second half with the same two-footed slam of moments before. The man hit the earth like a superhero.

Reuben followed. His legs gave out when he landed, and he fell forward, slamming his head against a steel handrail. Something rang like a bell. Either the railings or his brain. Hard to tell, and what did it matter anyway? He lost his breath when Danko reached over and grabbed the back of his collar, choking him as he pulled him to his feet. He dragged him away down the ramp.

A stuttered burst of firing bullets lit up their surroundings with a series of *tings!* They hit the old trains in the yard, steel containers, railings, and fences. But the drones were too far away, their shots woefully inaccurate.

Danko disappeared first, Reuben following him into the underground train station seconds later.

The space opened up into a subterranean amphitheatre. Metal stairs similar to the ones in the shopping mall led them lower. Cracked, off-white tiles covered the floor, walls, and ceiling. Danko crossed them, disturbing clouds of dust as he ran toward another set of old escalators that descended into a dark abyss.

Danko paused at the top and reached inside a panel on his left. Lights came on a few seconds later. He shrugged. "It'll give Fear's army something to follow, but we need it to guide us out of here."

Reuben fell into the same stride as his leader, their steps slamming down in stereo until they reached the bottom of the stairs, turned right through an archway, and burst onto an old platform. They halted instantly.

A pack of wild dogs gathered before them. A ragtag coalition of ten to fifteen mutts, they varied in size and shape, but every one of them welcomed the fight. Ten to fifteen pairs of receded lips. Ten to fifteen sets of sharp teeth, saliva dripping from some in long gooey strings. Several of them added to the collective low rumbling growl.

Danko dashed his baton against the ground. It landed on the concrete platform with a loud *crash* and skittered towards the creatures.

The dogs bolted.

"Thank fuck for—"

The stampede hitting the metal stairs of the escalators halted Reuben's relief.

Danko jumped from the platform to the tracks, landing on the large stones with a *crunch!* Two metal tracks, as true as the ones beneath the walkway, ran straight and parallel along their path. Concrete sleepers every few feet provided a level base for the rails, and stepping stones for Reuben and Danko. Had Danko not flicked on the lights, one of them would have broken an ankle within the first few minutes.

The acoustics of the underground station amplified and distorted Fear's pursuit. Hard to tell how close they were. It took for the first crunches of stones to pinpoint their location.

Reuben's already stinging eyes burned. He refused to blink, watching every step. Fear's army at their back, would they find the diseased ahead? What would they do if they ran in to a horde down here?

∽

It took them about three minutes at the most to reach the next station. Danko vaulted up onto the platform, and Reuben followed. They darted through another archway, heading for another abandoned escalator.

One flight of metal stairs led them out of there. The one that ran parallel to it had been destroyed beyond use.

Just a few feet behind Danko, and with the daylight flooding down into the station to guide him, Reuben ran up to the top of the stairs.

Once again, Danko stood aside to let him through. This time he turned off the lights. "That'll buy us some time."

But the second he turned to join Reuben, Danko halted. Drones hummed outside. They were waiting for them to exit. A hard stamp, Danko spoke through a clenched jaw. "Fuck!"

CHAPTER 31

Danko stamped his foot again, and he punched down with balled hands. "Fuck it!" He pressed the button on his wristband several times as if force and frequency would expedite the dogs' arrival. He shook his head. "I don't know how many dogs we've lost today. Or where they are in the city." He pointed at the escalators. "The lack of light down there will only slow Fear's army. They'll get up here soon enough."

The first steps hit the bottom of the escalators. The drones' hum continued to hover in wait. More soldiers began their ascent. The darkness might have slowed them, but Reuben and Danko couldn't block the daylight spilling in from the street above.

"Fuck!" Danko said again, standing on his tiptoes as if it would help him better assess the threat outside. He ran back to the top of the escalator. A hand on either rail, he stared down into the darkness and called over his shoulder to Reuben, "Watch out for the dogs. It sounds like there's only a few drones for now."

The first blue-uniformed soldier came into view. Danko

swung forwards and kicked her with both feet. She screamed as she returned to the darkness, hitting several soldiers behind her, eliciting a chorus of yells and thuds.

Whomp! The glow of fire spread down into the station. "They've arrived," Reuben said. "Let's get out of here."

Danko kicked another soldier back.

Reuben ran over to him and tugged on his arm. "Come on, let's go."

Another two soldiers broke from the darkness, and Danko kicked them one after the other. "You go," he said.

"*What?*"

"I'll make sure they don't follow." He slammed into another soldier with both feet. He hit the man hard enough to lift him from the stairs as he flew back. A few seconds later, the man landed with a *crunch*.

A wild scream lit a chill up Reuben's spine. It came from somewhere below. Reuben moved his mouth several times before the words came out. "Diseased!"

Fear's army shrieked. They ascended the stairs quicker than before.

"We can both get out of here," Reuben said.

"They won't open the gates if we have this many soldiers with us." Danko kicked the next soldier and then the next. "The second I turn my back, we'll be overwhelmed. You go. While you still can."

"I'm not a coward. I'll stay and fight."

More diseased joined the chorus in the dark tunnels below.

Danko's skin had turned pale. He gulped. The slightest shake of his head. "This is a losing battle." Another one-two kick. Another pair of soldiers returned from whence they came. "I once ran away and left someone when I could have stayed and fought. Had I remained, we would have won, and Lucie would have lived. I was a coward, so I know the coward's route." His voice broke. "This isn't it. We can't win this fight. Make the smart choice, Reuben. At least make sure one of us walks away from this." He shoved Reuben and turned to kick another soldier. "Go! Now!"

"Why don't you go? I'll stay and fight."

"You're better than me. You have more to offer this world. You saved those two civvies in the city when I wanted to kill them."

"You saw me do that?"

Danko kicked another soldier square in the man's solar plexus. "I was furious at the time, but it was the right choice. This war's bullshit. We gain nothing by killing everyone who's not like us. Walk away while you still can. While you still have a life that's worth something. Your duty should be to yourself, not this stupid city. They don't give a shit about you. Don't get dragged into it like I did. Don't become Sarge's puppet. Fury isn't worth dying for."

Danko kicked another soldier. This one caught his foot.

Reuben lunged at the blue-uniformed man, slamming the heel of his palm into his nose. He dragged Danko free.

Danko twisted away from Reuben and stumbled backwards. "Even if we get back to Fury"—he tapped his temple with his right index finger—"I can't run from what's in here. I'm done. I'm tired. Too much has already happened that I can't undo. I've done things I can't change. And I will continue to do things I'm not proud of. It's what I am now, and I'm ready for it to end." He shoved Reuben for a second time. "Now go, new boy, and find a life with meaning. Go find something better than this. This is for Lucie. This is what I should have done all those years ago." Danko charged down the stairs, drew his knife from the back of his trousers, and yelled. Before he vanished into the darkness, he leaped, knife first.

Reuben froze. The soldiers screamed from Danko's

attack. The diseased in the tunnels wailed. What would he gain if he followed him? Another *whomp* of a fireball, the dogs and drones remained locked in battle above.

If Reuben waited any longer, he'd miss his moment. Exhaustion and grief ran through his veins like molasses. His heart about ready to break. His lungs tight. His eyes sore. His uniform clung to his sweat-soaked body. He clamped his jaw, yelled to will himself forwards, and charged up the stairs, exiting the underground station.

CHAPTER 32

Unlike when he'd returned alone previously, the large steel gates opened on Reuben's approach. And a good job too. Making him knock this time would have been the final straw. Although, he'd already made up his mind. Danko had been right to warn him away from this place. Fuck this city and all it stood for. Their army was nothing but fodder for a pointless war without end. A political lever to show the people how the government protected them. And in exchange for said protection, they took control.

Every blink burned. His tears stung his sore eyes like he cried acid. They'd lost many excellent soldiers today, but not a single ounce of his grief had been for Hicks. Some people deserved to die. But Danko, while a complete lunatic, and someone who'd committed heinous acts, hadn't chosen to break as completely as he had. And Hernandez, she'd been nothing but kind. Groves ... His grief lurched through him in another all-consuming wave, snapping him forwards at the waist. Another rush of stinging tears. He heaved, but his stomach was empty. His stomach and his heart. A black hole occupied his chest. Something beyond loss. Utter vacancy. A tangible nothing. A vacuous mass ringing with an echoing reminder of absence. A projection of the future he'd never have. Better to have loved and lost ... Not if it felt like this.

His usual walk where he held his hands behind his back and his brow locked in a scowl. Sarge's eyes narrowed as he emerged from Fury's gates. "Where is everyone?"

The first thing he fucking asked. Where is everyone? Reuben spat his reply. "Where do you think?" Fuck Sarge and his shitty cause. Fuck everything he stood for. Reuben's voice came out louder than he'd intended. His words rasped. "They're all dead."

Still ten feet from Reuben, Sarge halted. His taut frame sagged. "*All* of them?"

"And for what? What did we achieve?" Reuben used his fingers to list the fallen. "Hicks, Hernandez, Danko, G ..." Her name died in his throat. Died in his heart. "Groves. Gone too. All of them."

"And the other units?"

Reuben shook with the force of his words. "*All* of them!"

Sarge's stoicism wavered. His mouth fell and his stubbled jaw hung loose in the wind. He shook his head, his voice softening. "I'm so sorry."

Sorry for what? For their loss? For his loss? For the logistical nightmare he now faced. Where would they get the new bodies from to sacrifice for their cause?

"I'm sorry for what you've had to go through. No one should have to experience that in their first few weeks. But you've survived. That's no mean feat. You clearly have what it takes."

That brief sentence. Those six words ran straight to Reuben's heart. The praise he'd wanted to hear from this man since childhood. He'd made the grade. He'd lived up to expectation.

The moment passed when Sarge's militant demeanour returned. He stamped his right foot and saluted. "You've earned yourself a promotion, soldier. We'll put you with another team for the next few weeks, but when the new wave of rookies come through, you'll be leading a unit. You're one of my guys now." He spread his arms wide.

Reuben stepped towards Sarge and fell into the man's firm embrace. He'd never smelled him before, although he'd imagined it. The undertones of sweat and something else. Something he couldn't place. Something musty. The scent of a man. Another pang stabbed through him. The aroma of absence, of a male role model he'd never had. Of the life he'd yearned for. He'd been waiting most of his life to say the words. "Thanks, Dad."

For the briefest of seconds, Sarge squeezed harder.

"I've always wanted you in my life," Reuben said. "Mum would be so happy to see this right now."

The hug could have gone on forever and it wouldn't have lasted long enough. An empty well that needed filling. When Sarge broke away and stepped back, Reuben leaned towards him. But he had to be patient. More would come. They'd reconnected. They had so much to talk about. But not here. Not now. They had the rest of their lives ahead of them. They had years to make up for lost time.

Sarge slammed a hard slap against Reuben's back while ushering him inside the gates. "Now go on, soldier, go home and get some rest. We'll send you out on the morning shift tomorrow. You're my guy now. Don't forget that."

But the warmth of his dad's hug could only last so long. As Reuben passed him and headed back to his home, to his one-room bedsit and his picture of his mother, the absence of his father turned him cold. The absence of Groves. Of Hernandez. Of Danko, the crazy lunatic. The black hole opened up again inside him. A black hole he couldn't ever fill, no matter how many pats on the back and well dones he received. But they needed to teach Fear's army a lesson. For what they'd done to Groves. This war had to end so they couldn't do it again to anyone else. As the leader of a new unit, he'd be the one to help make that happen.

CHAPTER 33

"Thank you for your service." The little boy wrung his hands and focused on his feet. His scruffy brown hair danced in the wind.

Reuben smiled. "Thank you."

"I-I-I …" The boy paused as if to reset himself. His roving gaze never landed on Reuben.

"It's okay," Reuben said, bending down to be at eye level with the boy. He rested a hand on the kid's shoulder. "Take your time."

"I want to serve in the military when I'm older."

The words slammed into Reuben, and he thrust his arms out to maintain his balance. The same thing he might have said as a boy. He gulped, his throat tight. He nodded several times, glancing over at the boy's parents. They stood grinning, another child in their arms. An infant. Would she have the same ambitions as her big brother? But who knows, things might be different by the time they reached the age required to serve? They might have moved on. Might have won the war. And Reuben could be in a place to make that happen. If he stood for what he believed in, and with his dad at his side, he could reshape their future. He could help Fury live up to its greatness. "Can I give you one piece of advice?"

For the first time, the boy made eye contact. His blue eyes were clear. Stark in their purity. It took Reuben a few seconds to find his words. "*Never* compromise who you are. Whatever happens, don't lose sight of that and you'll be okay." He ruffled the kid's hair and saluted him. "Now on your way, soldier."

The kid saluted back, cracked his heels together, and returned to his mum and dad with a skipping run.

~

Reuben arrived at the front gates with a few minutes to spare, his uniform clean and pressed like it had been on his first day. A new beginning. A fresh start. The morning sun burned bright in the near-cloudless sky. Things would be different from now on.

Sarge stood on his tiptoes at Reuben's approach and waved him over. Reuben waved back, smiled, and ran to the man in what came damn close to a skipping run. "Hi, D—"

"You're going out with Fox and her crew today."

The man's words slammed through Reuben. His familiar scowl had returned. Disdain tainted his features. Revulsion. "Yesterday was a fucking disaster—"

"But, D—"

"Make sure it doesn't happen again."

Reuben had been a fool to think things had changed between them. He'd set his expectations too high. Of course he'd be let down. What did he expect? His dad specialised in disappointment.

Fox, a short and squat woman in her early thirties,

snarled at Reuben and hooked a thumb over her shoulder. "Get to the back of the line. I'm not happy about taking you out. It seems like people die when you're around."

Sarge snorted a laugh. "He even killed the girl he had a crush on. No one's safe with this disaster of a soldier. This is a big test for you. You'll do well to straighten him out."

Reuben stumbled back a pace, his arm across his stomach as if it would somehow protect him from the verbal assault.

"Know that if I get even a sniff of you fucking up"—Fox pointed at him—"I'm leaving you for dead."

Like he'd done with Danko, Sarge threw a paternal arm around Fox and turned away from Reuben while he muttered, "Fucking rookies. So many of them are a waste of space."

Reuben went to the back of the line. He passed a soldier he'd seen signing up on his first day. She sneered as if she outranked him. So much for Fury needing him. So much for making him a leader. So much for him forcing change from the inside. Had he screwed up in calling Sarge dad too soon?

"Now, we've had a few rough days," Sarge said, his hands behind his back, his familiar march up and down in front of the soldiers. He walked as if yesterday hadn't happened. They'd lost tens of soldiers, and he carried on as normal. They'd lost Groves out there. A daughter and a sister. "Fury needs a win today. We see any of Fear's soldiers, we need to show them what for. We need to make sure they know what it means to be at war with us."

Many of the leaders nodded their agreement. Some slammed fists against their chests.

The red flag of their city in his grip, Sarge punched the air. "For Fury!"

The soldiers' response bounced back at them from the vast wall. "For Fury!"

Fox's unit was the second in line. She led them towards the open gates. As she passed Sarge, the man winked at her, turning his attention to the next team leader before Reuben got close enough to be acknowledged.

The will to run, to keep up with his unit and fight in this war drained from Reuben. The weight of his surname, the burden that had crushed him since he'd been old enough to understand it, tugged on his frame. Reuben Never. As in he'd *never* get Sarge's surname. The product of a one-night stand with a whore. The reminder that because Sarge couldn't keep it in his pants, he'd been lumbered with the consequences. Reuben had become the personification of Sarge's mistake, and his dad would never love him like he loved the military.

Fox led her team down an alley on her right. Reuben turned left.

"Hey, rookie!" Fox paused in the alley, her team backing up behind her. "Where the fuck do you think you're going?"

Reuben ripped his shirt open. The buttons burst free, and the fabric tore. He shrugged it off and threw it on the ground before spitting on it. "My life is worth more than this shitty war. You lead your team to their death if you like, but I won't do it anymore. I'm done."

"You'd best not try coming back to the city, rookie. Not after this."

Reuben had already turned his back on her. Why would he want to live in a city that had claimed the life of the first girl he'd ever loved? Where his mum had died. Where his dad was the biggest arsehole in the place, and where they treated their veterans like their service meant nothing. Fury chewed people up and spat them out. If they didn't die outside the walls, they'd sink into a slow and humiliating decline inside. Either way, what did he have to fight for?

Around the next bend, Reuben's unit were now out of sight. How long would it take Malcom to find the note he'd left for him in his bedsit? The keys to his home. All he asked was he took care of his mum. Flowers once in a while and say good morning and good night to her. He'd left the picture of her behind. He'd left everything behind. He'd set it all up the previous evening as the warmth from his interaction with his father cooled. By the morning, he expected the man to be an arsehole when he saw him next. Although, Sarge had surpassed even his lowest expectations. And of course he'd prayed things had changed, but his dad hadn't given him a single reason to stay.

In his note, Reuben had thanked Malcolm for being the father he wished he'd had. And that he didn't mourn the absence of Sarge because Malcolm had been there for him. But despite how much he loved the man, and how much he valued his friendship, Reuben wouldn't, and couldn't, come back to Fury. To live in that city after everything that had gone on would be to give up on who he was. He couldn't fight in a war he didn't believe in. Fear's soldiers were just like them. They didn't deserve to die. Whatever the world had in store, be it hordes of diseased or a swift execution at the hand of another army, it had to be better than playing a part in his fucked-up society.

Another unit passed him as he removed his trousers. He wore his civvy clothes beneath. He discarded the last shred of the uniform he'd waited years to wear. His dreams might have been shattered, but at least he now understood the truth. The people of Fury feared the diseased, but the living were a thousand times worse.

He'd head north. He'd heard life moved slower up there, as long as you could avoid the diseased. Maybe he'd find a friendly city with a simpler existence. A place where they valued their citizens. Somewhere with less violence. And if not, he'd rather die than remain a citizen of Fury.

. . .

The End.

Thank you for reading *Fury: Book one of Tales From Beyond These Walls.*

While this book is a standalone story, it exists at the same time as book eight in my *Beyond These Walls* series.

To find out more information about Beyond These Walls, go to - www.michaelrobertson.co.uk

Please see my 'Also by' section for a list of all the books in the series. But as a starting point, if you're yet to check out my *Beyond These Walls* series, you can get book one: *Protectors* at www.michaelrobertson.co.uk

Alternatively, you can make a saving by getting the books 1 - 6 box set.

Support The Author

Dear reader, as an independent author I don't have the resources of a huge publisher. If you like my work and would like to see more from me in the future, there are two things you can do to help: leaving a review, and a word-of-mouth referral.

Releasing a book takes many hours and hundreds of dollars. I love to write, and would love to continue to do so. All I ask is that you leave an Amazon review. It shows other readers that you've enjoyed the book and will encourage them to give it a try too. The review can be just one sentence, or as long as you like.

∽

If you've enjoyed Beyond These Walls, you might also enjoy my other post-apocalyptic series. The Alpha Plague: Books 1-8 (The Complete Series) are available now.

The Alpha Plague - Available Now

Or save money by picking up the entire series box set.

THE ALPHA PLAGUE - CHAPTER ONE

Alice pressed her fork down on her steak. The soft meat leaked a pool of blood that spread over her white plate. It soaked into the potatoes and broccoli.

A slow heave lifted in her throat, and she gulped several times to combat the excess saliva that gushed into her mouth. She could almost taste the metallic tang of blood. "How was the—" another heave rose up and she cleared it with a cough that echoed through the sparse room. She tried again. "How was the lab today, John?"

A thick frown furrowed John's brow. This was his usual response to most questions. Everything was an irritation. Such banal conversations couldn't hold a flame to his vast intellect. He ejected the word as if giving a reply was below him. "Stressful."

The rejection sent a sharp stab through Alice's stomach. It didn't matter how many times he knocked her down, she got back up and continued to look for his approval. Fire spread beneath her cheeks and she chewed on her bottom lip.

John flashed a grin of wonky teeth. It took all of Alice's strength not to flinch at the ghastly sight. "I must say though, it's been made a little easier by Wilfred having to make me this meal."

A deep breath filled Alice's sinuses with the smell of disinfec-

tant; the smell she associated with John. Decades immersed in the study of bacteria and disease had driven his level of cleanliness to the point where it bordered on obsessive-compulsive. A frown darkened her view of the room. "What did you say the bet was?"

"I didn't."

Alice looked into his sharp blue eyes and waited for him to say more.

He didn't.

A look first at the man, dressed in his white lab coat, she then looked around at his white, minimalist penthouse apartment. Everything had a place, and everything was necessary. Beakers and test tubes littered the sides like ornaments. She hadn't ever seen a photograph on display, despite this being his personal space... no room for sentimentality here.

Alice squirmed in her seat as the silence swelled.

John watched her.

No matter how long she'd known the man for, John always made her itch in her own skin. As if pressured to break the overwhelming void between them, she said, "So, what was the bet about?"

"An experiment. I predicted the correct result."

A machine would have been better company. Alice frowned at him again and sighed.

"Oh, do pull yourself together, woman," John said. "You've got to learn to stop being so bloody sensitive."

*Despite his obnoxious behaviour, the man did have redeeming qualities. When he worked, his creativity and passion flowed from him. Science drove him like a heartbeat, but Alice couldn't excuse him time and again. She couldn't ignore every time he'd humiliated her during a lecture; every time he'd not let her finish her point; every time he'd selected her to clean the lab at the end of the day while he let his other students leave. "How about you learn to stop being so bloody **in**sensitive?"*

A flick of his bony hand at her and he said, "This is what I mean. It's these emotional fluctuations that take away your ability to be objective. That's why men make better scientists."

"And terrible companions."

He lowered his head and peered over his glasses at her. "We can leave our baggage at the door," he continued.

For the second time, her face smouldered. "You left your baggage in the delivery ward, John. Maybe your sociopathic detachment serves you well in the world of science, but it doesn't equip you to deal with the real world. Without science, you'd be stranded." Her vision blurred. Great! Tears again. They only strengthened the man's argument.

John sighed and shook his head.

A glance down at her dinner, and Alice prodded the soft steak. Maybe a scalpel would be more appropriate than the wooden-handled knife in her hand. In the bright glare of John's scrutiny, Alice cut into the steak and lifted a piece to her mouth.

The soft meat sat like jelly on her tongue. Unable to chew it, she took a deep gulp and tried to swallow. The piece of steak stuck in her throat like it was barbed. Her heart raced as a metallic rush of juices slithered down her oesophagus and clogged her throat.

John watched on, his expression unchanged. The cold detachment of a scientist rather than the compassion of a human being stared through his beady eyes.

Alice's pulse boomed inside her skull. She held her neck and wheezed, "Help me."

He didn't. He believed in natural selection. Sink or swim. How many cavemen had choked on their dinner? The ones who had been saved only weakened the gene pool. Weakness should never be rewarded.

After several heavy gulps, Alice swallowed the meat, leaned on the table, and gasped. Adrenaline surged through her. Her pulse pounded in her ears. She dabbed her eyes with the back of her hand to stop her mascara from running and looked up to see John watching her with his usual blank expression. A barrage of abuse rose and died on her tongue; there was no point.

Alice retuned her focus to her dinner and flinched every time her cutlery hit the porcelain plate. The sharp chinks bounced around the quiet room. After she'd cut everything up, she stared at her food. A tightness remained in her throat from when she'd choked; another sip of warm red wine did little to ease her trepidation.

When she looked back up, John still watched her.

She cleared her throat. "So, when will you tell me about your work, John?"

His dinner remained untouched; his scrawny frame and pallid skin served as a visual representation of his poor diet. Thirty years her senior at sixty-three, he looked fifty years older. He consulted his wristwatch as if their meal had a deadline and sighed. "I can't. You know that."

While she watched him, she speared some potato and put it in her mouth, chewed, and took another sip of wine. The fluffy vegetable disintegrated and slid down her throat when she swallowed. Eating under John's cold scrutiny seemed to increase the possibility that she'd choke again. Maybe he was right; maybe her tension was all in the mind.

She ate a piece of purple sprouting broccoli. The bland vegetable had taken on the rich tang of blood from the steak.

Despite the slow heave that turned through her stomach again, Alice focused hard on mastication. When the food had no taste left, she swallowed the weak mush.

When she looked up again, the strip lighting sent electric shocks through her eyeballs. She shielded her brow as she looked at John. "Have the lights gotten brighter?"

John didn't respond.

"The lights," she repeated as she viewed the room through slits. "Have they been turned up?" Her world blurred, and the beginnings of a migraine stretched its poisonous roots through her brain.

Alice changed the subject. "I know you can't tell me about your work, John. It's just, as my professor, I long to understand more. You're here to teach me, after all." Another sharp pain jabbed into her eyes, and she drew a short breath that echoed in the bare room. While she stared down at the white table, she pinched her forehead for relief.

"Are you okay?" His tone showed no evidence of concern. It seemed more like someone on a scientific quest to collate information. She expected to look up and see him taking notes. John didn't believe in downtime. The world should be viewed through objective eyes at all times. Emotions belonged to the irrational.

Two hollow knocks sounded out when John dropped his pointy elbows on the table. Alice looked up to see his long and bony fingers entwine. His deep and languid voice rumbled, "Eat more, it will make you feel better. As for my work, you'll have to keep wondering, I'm afraid. Since the Second Cold War started with The East, everything has been on a need-to-know basis."

"The Second Cold War? That's always your excuse, John. Since the terrorist attacks in 2023–"

"And the second wave a year later." He spoke to her as if she didn't know her history. He spoke to her as if she barely knew her own name.

A deep breath helped her withhold her retort. "The point I was trying to make," she said, "is that nothing's happened for the last fifteen years. We've had the silent threat of war hanging over us like a thick fog. Sometimes I wonder whether it's just a way for the government to take our civil liberties away. I wouldn't be surprised if they put a Doomsday Clock in every city just to remind us of how much protection we need. Just so we obey their every wish."

"Don't be ridiculous, Alice. You sound like one of those new-age paranoid types."

"As opposed to the old-age paranoid types? At least my beliefs don't result in us stockpiling weapons of mass destruction." Fire spread across her face and she trembled. Years of repressed argu-

ments always rushed forward when things got tense between them. One day he'd get the lot, regardless of whether he labelled her irrational or not.

His long features twisted, but he remained silent.

"Besides, when you're connected to those in power, I'm sure it does seem preposterous. You'll be okay, John; you have a space in their fallout shelters when you want it. Ironic really."

"What is?"

She gasped when her stomach lurched. She coughed several times before she said, "The fact that the wealthy and privileged will survive if it all goes to hell, left to remake the world in their own greedy image. I mean,"—she forced a laugh that fell dead in the sparse room—"that's what got us in this state in the first place. It would seem that humanity is destined to repeat itself if they're the people who will crawl out of the ground after this planet has been ravaged by a nuclear war." A huge gulp of wine, and she slammed the glass back down on the table. When she pulled her hair from her face, the light in the room hit her like sharp needles fired into her eyeballs.

A gentle slur dampened her words, and the warm liquid that she'd tried to drink dribbled down her chin. "Anyway, maybe we'll work together when I graduate."

When she looked back up, she saw regret in his cold eyes. The flicker of emotion sat awkwardly on his stony face. "Maybe," he allowed. "How's your food? Wilfred is quite the chef, don't you think?"

If Wilfred never cooked again it would be too soon. Alice didn't reply.

John maintained the silence.

No matter how much she wriggled, Alice found no comfort on the hard plastic chair. Sweat dampened her back. Before she spoke, she paused. The words had abandoned her, so she fished in her increasingly foggy mind for them. The first three words came out as a slur, "Yes, he is. However, the steak is a little rare for my liking." A hard throb surged through her temples. She drew a sharp breath through her clenched teeth and slapped her hands to her face. When she pushed against her eyeballs, it did nothing to ease her pain; they felt ready to burst.

John showed little concern. After he'd regarded his watch again, he lifted a small black box and pressed a button on it. "I agree. Wilfred likes his meat bloody." He said the word like a vampire with a thirst. "This is well done by his standards."

A gentle whir sounded, and darkness fell over the room.

When Alice twisted her head, she saw heavy metal shutters close over the windows. "When were they fitted?" she asked. Her own words echoed through her mind.

A half smile twisted John's face. "Earlier today."

Every beat of her pulse kicked her brain. Her stomach tensed. She stammered, "W... why are you... um, why are you locking us in?"

His laugh echoed through her skull and her world spun. "I'm not locking us in, dear. I'm locking them out. We've had information that suggests the Cold War may heat up tonight. We believe that China and Korea have mastered biological warfare. This apartment is already well fortified; I've just added the shutters to prevent an airborne virus from entering." As if in afterthought, he added, "I'm sure that nothing will happen, but it's better to be safe."

Fire barrelled through her guts. Sweat gushed from her brow, and the thick black bars of tunnel vision shut off her peripheral sight. Everything fell into soft focus. She felt disconnected from the words as she said them. "Oh, so we have to stay here?" Several blinks did nothing to clear her vision.

With a sombre nod, John said, "Yes. We have plenty of rations though."

Where? The apartment had seemed empty—not that she could see much now; maybe she'd missed a stash of supplies.

Another rush of heat forced sweat from every pore. John

vanished from her view as his white coat blended into the surroundings.

Alice wheezed. "Is that why you're checking your watch? You know when it's supposed to happen?"

Before John replied, everything went dark and she fell sideways. Sharp pain exploded across her cheek as she hit the table. The smell of bleach slithered up her nostrils.

"It won't be long now, dear."

She heard his chair scrape across the floor.

"Would you excuse me while I go and use the bathroom? I want to make the most of that luxury because we'll need to stay in this room from here on out. It'll be a bucket in the corner after thisssssssss…"

His words faded as her vision failed her.

⁓

THE SUN SHONE DIRECTLY INTO RHYS' eyes when he pulled up outside Dave's house. On the first attempt, he flapped at the sun visor and missed it, the glare so strong it blinded him. The thing creaked when he flipped it down on the second attempt. The car was a relic, but it wasn't like he could afford anything else. When the custody battle for his boy was finally over with, he'd get one of the latest models. The Audi Aurore had automatic sun visors as standard from the 2035 model onwards. It may be a few years old, but something like that would be much nicer than the twenty-year-old Peugeot piece of shit he had to drive.

He left the engine running to keep the air conditioner on. Dave wouldn't be out straight away, and Rhys refused to cook in the car while he waited.

Nauseous dread sat in Rhys' stomach as it did every Monday morning. As clichéd as it was to hate Mondays, Rhys couldn't fucking stand them. They served as a sharp reminder that another weekend had passed where he hadn't seen his son.

A quick toot of the horn, and he leaned back in his seat to wait.

~

Rhys checked his watch for the sixth time, at least; a minute had passed, maybe more. The cool air blew on Rhys' face. It stung his eyes slightly as the prolonged jet dried them out while he stared at Dave's blue front door. Rhys expected him to be late, but he'd usually acknowledged Rhys' presence by now. Dishevelled hair and bleary eyes would have normally poked their head out of the door and winced the usual apology of the perpetually late, but he got nothing today.

Another check of his watch, and Rhys tooted the horn again.

Dave 'ten more minutes' Allen always needed ten more minutes. They now had an agreement in place; Dave could have ten more minutes, but once that time had elapsed, Rhys left for work with or without him. At thirty-five, Dave could take responsibility for getting himself to work on time. Rhys often felt like his fucking mother.

~

Seven minutes left of the ten and still no sign of Dave. The corners of Rhys' eyes itched as he continued to watch Dave's front door. A quick check in the rear-view mirror, and he saw his own scowl. No wonder his eyes ached. Maybe he should just go now. Sod ten minutes. Dave can find his own damn way to work.

A heavy sigh, and Rhys shook his head. He couldn't do that, no matter how much he wanted to… not with their agreement in place. He reached up to press the horn again, but before he had the chance to, a loud *bang* crashed into the window next to him.

Rhys' heart leaped into his throat and he spun around to find himself face to face with the messy-haired Dave. His afro looked like a bird's nest. "What the fuck, man?" Not that he needed to ask; the stubble and bloodshot eyes told Rhys exactly what Dave had been up to. When he wound the window down, the heat of the morning rushed into the car with the reek of stale booze. Surprise, surprise.

"I'm sorry, mate," Dave said.

Rhys looked past Dave at the house he'd just left. Like Dave's house, it provided affordable living for the young professional. "You fucked Julie again?"

A half smile, and Dave shrugged. "How long have I got before you leave?"

After a glance down at the dash, Rhys said, "Four minutes." He had six, but Dave always needed the wiggle room.

Without another word, Dave jogged toward his house. A sprint would have no doubt reproduced most of the consumed alcohol from the previous night, and Rhys didn't need to see that, even if it did mean Dave moved slower.

The electric window whirred as Rhys did it up again, and the leather seat groaned when he leaned back into it. Despite the cool air conditioning, the heat of the sun warmed his face, and he closed his eyes. One day, Dave would surprise him by being on time.

Yeah, right.

∼

When Dave opened the car door, Rhys opened his eyes again. A glance at the clock, and he quickly sat upright. The cheeky fucker had taken twelve minutes from him; it best not fuck things up for seeing his boy. The opportunities for him to see Flynn were few and far between. The last thing he needed was Dave ruining that, even though he couldn't ever know what time to pass Flynn's school because his mother was so damn inconsistent. When they'd been together, Larissa kept time like an army sergeant. Now she turned up whenever she fucking liked. She used it as a way to fuck with him, a way of repeated punishment for his one mistake.

"Sorry again, mate," Dave said as he strapped his seatbelt on. "I don't have my alarm at Julie's."

Rhys made a quick check over his shoulder and signalled before he pulled away. Being pissed with him wouldn't help, but Rhys couldn't let go of the tension that gripped his jaw. Not that he could really blame Dave; he could have left him after ten minutes like they'd previously agreed.

A deep sigh, and Rhys rolled his shoulders. It loosened the tension slightly. "What's going on with you two? That's the fifth time in the past fortnight that you've stayed over there."

"You know what it's like, mate; we go out on the piss, bump into each other all drunk and horny, one thing leads to another…"

"Why don't you just start dating her? You're thirty-five now, Dave, you ain't getting any younger."

"Exactly."

Rhys raised an eyebrow at him. "Huh?"

"I have less time left in my life," Dave explained. "Do you seriously think I need to fill what's left of whatever existence I have with the bullshit of being attached to somebody? I like fucking; I don't like going to garden centres on a Sunday and picking out potted plants. Besides, you're hardly a shining example to follow when it comes to relationships."

"That was below the belt, mate."

"Tell me I'm wrong."

Rhys shook his head. "Whatever."

"Do you remember when you were out on the weekends with us? The wild nights on the town with the boys?"

Of course he remembered them. The hint of a smile lifted his lips.

Despite his apparent lethargy, Dave jumped on it. "See? They were fun times... bullshit chat up lines that worked more often than not, a different woman every night, dancing until the early hours, and a takeaway on the way home. When you wake up in a strange bed with a naked woman and a half-eaten kebab in your pocket, you knew you'd had a good night. How's that not fun?"

When they rounded the next bend, the sun shone directly into the front of the car. The glare burned Rhys' eyes, but it seemed like nothing compared to Dave. First he shrieked, hid behind his forearms, and then flapped around until he'd found his sunglasses and slipped them on.

"What are you," Rhys said, "a fucking vampire?"

"The hangovers get harder with each passing week, man. I'm getting too old for this."

"Yeah, I don't miss that."

"You should come out with us one weekend. I know the boys would be pleased to see you."

"I would," Rhys said, "but I have different priorities now. I'm a dad and I need to behave like one. I may have troubles with Larissa, but Flynn is my reason for being. I need to do the right thing by him."

The route to work always passed Flynn's school. Of course, Rhys wanted to arrive at work on time, but he lived for the chance to pass Flynn when he got dropped off at the gates. Just one glance of his little boy could keep him going for a week or more.

When they got close, Rhys slowed down and looked across at all the children. Dave shut up as Rhys continued to search. Between eight and nine, all of the kids got dropped off by their parents; a quick glance at the clock on the dash showed him it was eight twenty-three.

∼

Even after they'd passed the primary school, Rhys continued to look over his shoulder. Not that it served any purpose; there were only a handful of kids, and most of them were girls.

As Rhys sped up, Dave rubbed his temples and reclined into his seat again. "No Flynn today?"

Did it look like Flynn was there today? Rhys pushed out a heavy sigh to try to force some of his frustration away. "No, I swear she drops him at a different time every day just to fuck with me. All I want is a small glance of him, a wave before I go to work. I just want him to know how much I love him. I don't want him to forget me. Instead, I feel like a fucking stalker… a nonce that slows down and stares at the children going into school." With his jaw clenched, he added, "I swear she gets some sick pleasure from it."

It may have been a clumsy hand, guided by an exhausted and clearly still intoxicated man, but when Dave squeezed Rhys' shoulder, it sent a shimmer of sadness through his heart. The sting of tears itched his eyeballs, and he continued to stare straight ahead.

"He won't forget you, mate. Six year olds know who their parents are, even if they're separated. When did you see him last?"

"About a week and a half ago."

"So Saturday's your next day with him?"

With a grip so tight on the wheel it hurt his hands, Rhys' breathed quicker. "That's the plan. If she doesn't fucking cancel, that is."

"She's still cancelling a lot?"

"Yeah, whenever she damn well feels like it."

Dave let go of Rhys' shoulder, leaned back, and shook his head. "What a bitch."

Rhys didn't reply.

Thank you for reading The Alpha Plague Chapter One.

The Alpha Plague: Books 1-8 (The Complete Series) are available now.

The Alpha Plague - Available Now

Or save money by picking up the entire series box set.

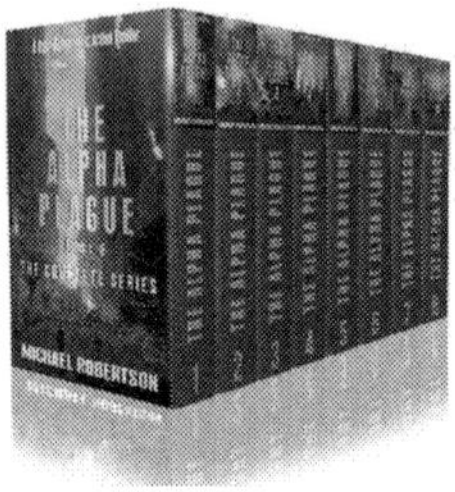

ABOUT THE AUTHOR

Like most children born in the seventies, Michael grew up with Star Wars in his life, along with other great stories like Labyrinth, The Neverending Story, and as he grew older, the Alien franchise. An obsessive watcher of movies and consumer of stories, he found his mind wandering to stories of his own.

Those stories had to come out.

He hopes you enjoy reading his work as much as he does creating it.

Contact
www.michaelrobertson.co.uk
subscribers@michaelrobertson.co.uk

READER GROUP

Join my reader group for all my latest releases and special offers. You'll also receive these four FREE books. You can unsubscribe at any time.

Go to www.michaelrobertson.co.uk

FURY - BOOK ONE OF TALES FROM BEYOND THESE WALLS

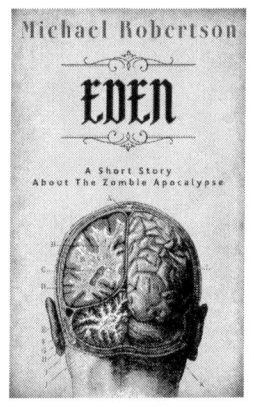

ALSO BY MICHAEL ROBERTSON

THE SHADOW ORDER:

The Shadow Order

The First Mission - Book Two of The Shadow Order

The Crimson War - Book Three of The Shadow Order

Eradication - Book Four of The Shadow Order

Fugitive - Book Five of The Shadow Order

Enigma - Book Six of The Shadow Order

Prophecy - Book Seven of The Shadow Order

The Faradis - Book Eight of The Shadow Order

The Complete Shadow Order Box Set - Books 1 - 8

∽

NEON HORIZON:

The Blind Spot - A Cyberpunk Thriller - Neon Horizon Book One.

Prime City - A Cyberpunk Thriller - Neon Horizon Book Two.

Bounty Hunter - A Cyberpunk Thriller - Neon Horizon Book Three.

Connection - A Cyberpunk Thriller - Neon Horizon Book Four.

Neon Horizon - Books 1 - 3 Box Set - A Cyberpunk Thriller.

∽

THE ALPHA PLAGUE:

The Alpha Plague: A Post-Apocalyptic Action Thriller

The Alpha Plague 2

The Alpha Plague 3

The Alpha Plague 4

The Alpha Plague 5

The Alpha Plague 6

The Alpha Plague 7

The Alpha Plague 8

The Complete Alpha Plague Box Set - Books 1 - 8

∽

BEYOND THESE WALLS:

Protectors - Book one of Beyond These Walls

National Service - Book two of Beyond These Walls

Retribution - Book three of Beyond These Walls

Collapse - Book four of Beyond These Walls

After Edin - Book five of Beyond These Walls

Three Days - Book six of Beyond These Walls

The Asylum - Book seven of Beyond These Walls

Between Fury and Fear - Book eight of Beyond These Walls

Before the Dawn - Book nine of Beyond These Walls

Beyond These Walls - Books 1 - 6 Box Set

∽

TALES FROM BEYOND THESE WALLS:

Fury - Book one of Tales From Beyond These Walls

∽

OFF-KILTER TALES:

The Girl in the Woods - A Ghost's Story - Off-Kilter Tales Book One

Rat Run - A Post-Apocalyptic Tale - Off-Kilter Tales Book Two

∼

Masked - A Psychological Horror

∼

CRASH:

Crash - A Dark Post-Apocalyptic Tale

Crash II: Highrise Hell

Crash III: There's No Place Like Home

Crash IV: Run Free

Crash V: The Final Showdown

∼

NEW REALITY:

New Reality: Truth

New Reality 2: Justice

New Reality 3: Fear

∼

Audiobooks:

The Alpha Plague Audiobooks:

US - Audiobook for The Alpha Plague Books 1 - 3.

UK - Audiobook for The Alpha Plague Books 1 - 3.

Germany - Audiobook for The Alpha Plague Books 1 - 3.

France - Audiobook for The Alpha Plague Books 1 - 3.

US - Audiobook for The Alpha Plague Book 4.
UK - Audiobook for The Alpha Plague Book 4.
Germany - Audiobook for The Alpha Plague Book 4.
France - Audiobook for The Alpha Plague Book 4.

US - Audiobook for The Alpha Plague Book 5.
UK - Audiobook for The Alpha Plague Book 5.
Germany - Audiobook for The Alpha Plague Book 5.
France - Audiobook for The Alpha Plague Book 5.

US - Audiobook for The Alpha Plague Book 6.
UK - Audiobook for The Alpha Plague Book 6.
Germany - Audiobook for The Alpha Plague Book 6.
France - Audiobook for The Alpha Plague Book 6.

US - Audiobook for The Alpha Plague books 7 & 8 box set.
UK - Audiobook for The Alpha Plague books 7 & 8 box set.
Germany - Audiobook for The Alpha Plague books 7 & 8 box set.
France - Audiobook for The Alpha Plague books 7 & 8 box set.

Beyond These Walls Audiobooks

US - Audiobook for Beyond These Walls Books 1 - 3.
UK - Audiobook for Beyond These Walls Books 1 - 3.
Germany - Audiobook for Beyond These Walls Books 1 - 3.
France - Audiobook for Beyond These Walls Books 1 - 3.

US - Audiobook for Beyond These Walls Books 4 - 6.
UK - Audiobook for Beyond These Walls Books 4 - 6.
Germany - Audiobook for Beyond These Walls Books 4 - 6.
France - Audiobook for Beyond These Walls Books 4 - 6.

The Shadow Order Audiobooks

US - Audiobook for The Shadow Order Books 1 - 3.

UK - Audiobook for The Shadow Order Books 1 - 3.

Germany - Audiobook for The Shadow Order Books 1 - 3.

France - Audiobook for The Shadow Order Books 1 - 3.

The Shadow Order books 4 - 6 coming to audio soon.

Rat Run Audiobook:

US - Audiobook for Rat Run.

UK - Audiobook for Rat Run.

Germany - Audiobook for Rat Run.

France - Audiobook for Rat Run.

Crash Audiobooks

US - Audiobook for Crash.

UK - Audiobook for Crash.

Germany - Audiobook for Crash.

France - Audiobook for Crash.

US - Audiobook for Crash II.

UK - Audiobook for Crash II.

Germany - Audiobook for Crash II.

France - Audiobook for Crash II.

US - Audiobook for Crash III.

UK - Audiobook for Crash III.

Germany - Audiobook for Crash III.

France - Audiobook for Crash III.

US - Audiobook for Crash IV.

UK - Audiobook for Crash IV.

Germany - Audiobook for Crash IV.

France - Audiobook for Crash IV.

Crash V coming to audiobook soon.

Printed in Great Britain
by Amazon